The Virgin Sky

By

Adi Khan

The Sky

What is so magical about the sky above us? Is it her grand vastness that creates the fear among us, or is it an infinite sadness that showers a sphere that surrounds us? The cry of her wail seldom reaches our core and yet when it does, its sigh penetrates through our every pore. On this earth we stand today, millions have come and many more have gone, how many have looked at her and thought, she is still young and yet completely alone. We gaze at her deeply only twice in our lifetime, once when we are truly in the grip of fear, the other when we wish her clouds to sprinkle after they tear. Why is it that apart from this we don't seem to care? Is not her air we wish truly was all that we had to wear? Do we see beauty only in ourselves and we wish not that a little of it we must with her, share?

This day, a young girl's heart has asked of its self these very questions, deep from within have arisen radical decisions and in the breadth of just a few moments they have decided her life's intentions. As she gazes out of the giant windows before her eyes, Sarah cries out to a deep blue sea, "it is only within your mist that I can truly be free, only in the warmth of your thousand sun's will I find my soul's key and only in the depths of your songs can I become one with each moment to simply be." "Can you swim, young one", a voice speaks to her from deep within the waves? I cannot truly, yet I shall find a boat and be within you shortly" she replies. These are the times that are so vital in our lives, they come suddenly and without warning, soon they become our spiritual guides taking us with them to places unknown and mysterious, yet only from the new and daunting arise the most profound experiences.

Sarah stands this day in the presence of such a moment, it whispers to her that she shall soon enter new and difficult worlds, face forbidding horizons, and break insurmountable boundaries, this, a voice tells her a critical juncture in her journey through both space and time. After this moment neither shall remain the same and thunderous waves of the oceans she shall have to tame.

Sarah closes her eyes and her sight turns inwards to a thousand thoughts that slide downwards to embrace a shimmering of feelings present deep inside her heart. Both dance in this ecstasy of joy and form with each other, a bond of love. Soon from within, a true and pure innocence is born; it travels within her layers, until it arrives at her eyes. Here it declares, to survive I must make way and leave you with my caress on your face and in the arms of your sighs. Sarah opens her eyes and amongst her tears finds in the distance, the outlines of a majestic swing, with its outstretched arms a voice from inside sings, "I await voyager do not waste even a second, for such an invitation may never come again."

The Park

Seldom is it that fairies sleep in their flights of destiny. A spirit burns within them the fires of passion, hope and desire, all vibrations of a mystical symphony. There is in life no greater pleasure than peeling slowly through the great mystery; never should one thus be afraid of striving for their epiphany. Awake she is, with her eyes closed, lying in the belly of a giant, thundering across the sky's, overtaking continents and making vast distances the fallacies of ancient eyes. In contrast lays humanity, with eyes open, yet deep in slumber, waiting since forever for a final thunder. The whale of the seas then floats gently towards shore, it hangs its oars and bids farewell to its travelers as she awaits a many others for her next soar.

As she steps into a world completely new, a whiff of cold air brushes past the innocence of a young fairy and says "welcome, Sarah, your journey begins here, just remember, to be to yourself completely true". In the haze, arises some time after, a serene view. People of all ages, all colors, of different countries and nations mingle with each other just as different colors mix together in a teacup brew. Yet among all these, there are young angels with dreams of taming the sky very few.

Some time after, in the thickness of a forest, she finds herself lost in a crowd of soldiers, well dressed, determined and following each other in a queue. On the surface different, yet most breathe the same morning dew, young bankers lost in the materialism of their tailored attire, aggressive street hawkers staking the play ground for the next foolish buyer and corporate executives adorned with wealth, commanding their armies with a venomous ire. Successful they seem to Sarah in the present reality of their world, yet true happiness, she has seen on no face so far. Engines too, rotate, she thinks, at a set momentum each hour.

Thinking her way through the abyss, she feels in her midst, the breeze from a nearby garden, from within a voice says, "Within my arms you must hide, upon my grass you must slide, verily, there is so much more to my essence than your eyes confide." Here, the grass graces gently upon her earth, just as a mother caresses her newborn, the trees whisper their adoration for their leaves, just as a seasoned

3

sailor dreams of the fascination of his seas, men and women walk at ease, eager and patiently awaiting the next warmth of a heavenly breeze. "people from mighty cities and towns arrive here in my midst just to breathe a little from the essence of my gown," she says. Stunned into silence is young girl in this moment, as her eyes gaze upon each flower resembling the creation of the greatest artisan. "A world apart is this place," confessions of a young rafter say, "can I just stay here and forever within play?"

"An angel from afar you are, Sarah," the breeze replies, "yet, you must lay within only, once you experience the core of your clay. Go far and beyond in this land, light your every fire and fulfill your every desire, and at last when you tire, than come onto me, for it is only then, that you shall understand and truly admire."

The Road

By the coast of a vast continent floats a gentle river, it arches through villages, towns, and cottages, like the branches of an intricate feather, from the southern gates of Canada to the northern shores of Cuba, its rhythmic flow balances the varying shades of the weather. It carries with it, stories and allegories of an ancient past, stitching for the passionate traveler a suit from the finest leather. Its waves whisper their many songs as they traverse a million fates, just as the freshness of its breath challenges the souls of stubborn states.

They say once a hundred set out to conquer its allure, five survived only to die a little after from wanting more and more. A hundred less five then, its sign today, some would forever wish to live within the arms of its care. Cement and stones though are harder to fight then the purity of the morning air. To be a true seeker is to know there are myths and legends of old, which one must never fear to shear. Early in life we must learn, there will be moments here that shall be hard for us to bear. Sometimes on an endless road, we find with us certain moments, which dazzle us with their flair, they bring along feelings which touch us deeply, just like the drizzle when she glides to us delicately in the guise of a tear. A journey within another at times brings hearts from afar together, a bind of necessity it is and yet it melts many into one, forever.

From behind as from top the world seems so much clearer, a fog of mystery lifting as the world moves faster. A look at her mother and she senses the slow death of a flower, another towards her father and what exists is a lonely existence in an ancient tower. They say accidents happen only in events that are linked by eternal chains, how many coils of iron must have locked in place to bring about these moments which seem the signature of autumn rains? The world fly's by in a flash when riding in the backseat of a car, just as life herself which seldom stops to tell her passengers, the intensity of an hour. Such is our destiny in this world, where we strive mostly for people and things, we forget in this ride, the beauty of a moment which passes softly much like the flow of the wind that never stings.

Basking in the sunshine this day reclines an angel, who sees in her sights today, the outlines of a far greater tomorrow. In the freshness of her thoughts are fantasies, allegories and questions about a thousand mysteries, this day only, she reflects, selects and masterfully deflects, all queries thrown, meadows shown, painful histories sown, as she is in her moment now, in her zone.

The City

On the edge of a protruding thumb, lies a place which defies all meaning. This special space flirts with the nail as it does with the skin, masking its feelings and drowning in the observers dreaming, its rugged intensity can be felt only when within, just as man's true nature becomes transparent only when in a state of sin. From the far reaches of space we can see of it nothing, only when we come much closer, do we see something we feel is worth admiring, only when we grace her skin, can we feel her infinite sighing, it is only then, that we see in her shadows, images of ourselves, laughing and smiling.

The darkness of her night then, lends to the three a little of her devilry, she says to them, "Soon, I shall hoist you all into my palace and shower you with my chivalry." She talks as she sings, of the tapestry of a painting named Miami. Exhilarated by the sight, they turn to her to confide, "Verily, your majesty, you must show us something of this fantasy." "I shall," she thunders, "as soon as you undertake a pilgrimage of my mystery, walk my artistry, sing my sophistry and rent your souls to the pages of my history". "Never have our eyes been in such a dazzling city," they shout in unison. "Have you never before lived your destiny?" She questions, "We are here only because a fire begs to see her chimney", the two in front answer. "Then you must let her laugh in my cry, smile in my sigh and live in my high, she will not feel the tear in my eye until you give her in my arms, where she will for a little while die." "May we ask why" they question from the dark siren of the sky, "the cloth of ideas you so carefully sowed, you must let herself untie, if not she will only continue to live in you and her life will be nothing except a lie."

"I can feel something in this night, I have never before, my dream is to know you deeply, so that together far and away we may soar," says Sarah, to the darkness that surrounds her eye. The darkness glares, stares and flings in all directions, thousands of her airs, after what has been an eternity has an entity arrived that dares to be among her millions of layers.

She whispers softly in an innocent ear, "welcome Sarah, enter freely, for you shall fly in my shadows as you shall sigh with my ancient pharos, fear not a star in the vast sky, as for you I shall make each except one of them shy. In the morning I will take you to him and together you and I shall glide through his light just as an angel does when she has learnt to fly.

Twins

They ask how an infant barely seconds old in this world knows how she must salivate to yearn from her mother a little of her luscious silver, cradled in an aroma of innocence and basked in a glowing warmness, the newborn never tires of placing upon reclining mounds, its soft lips which moisten ever so softly after they taste the early flakes of approaching winters. The salutations of a new reality too bring such lofty invitations. To dwell in the magic of a new horizon is similar to an escape from the most deathly prison. To live a life wherein an inquisitive emotion has turned to passion reveals into the clouds has an entity finally arisen.

The first hundred hours in every new story pass ever so slowly, they pause in their frailty, alas, they might shatter some its glory. For a young girl traversing through life in her voyage for the skies, these are days that are fresh different and new. In moments such as these, time herself cries "soon, this fairy too shall fly into the sky, and we shall do nothing except cry and rue." "Have you moments of pleasure so few?" asks space from his twin, "So would you, she replies, if you could never share all you knew, for people of earth have of us both, a completely different view, for only a few among the billions know we are one and not two."

"Beware of what you say, for at times even a young girl can decipher what space and time together whisper," replies space to his sister. "Most have forgotten and yet not all are so pale in memory, for I remember being dust since eternity yet still a tiny grain in the depths of your symphony, the story of your birth as mine, I always knew, yet it is only now that I feel alive and true,"

"Together we have been since we breathed, Sarah and in perfect symmetry do we dazzle each other, we fight often, but we love even more, we travel different paths but of the trust we share, we are completely sure. You are now both innocent and pure and of the rock you glide upon you have much to know, as my other will share, her hands lead some to a life of content and flow yet many more to regret and despair, grief and sorrow is how we define your world, yet know deeply who you are and you shall feel with each passing second how close you are to a majestic shore."

"Cherish I shall then, the care you both gift, yet in my mind as in my heart I feel no fear, your love and your warmth I shall always treasure, for barely seconds have passed since we spoke and already my heart feels she can fly forever."

The Roar

Evenings pass by swiftly in the rhythmic beat of the new city. Mornings however are much heavier and prefer to walk in their journey. A few days have gone by rather quickly, others have sauntered through their way in the shadows of an unfolding mystery. Every now and then a few moments arise, which take us to heights and sights beyond our greatest boundaries, such is the importance of such a time, that a few seconds decide the destiny of our lives. In such a moment is present a young girl amid her guardians, who struggle like many others to understand their starlets wishes and desires, "What is it, Sarah?" A mother asks her daughter, her father follows, an observer of nature, but a failed actor in this picture, "Where are you going, Sarah?" he manages softly.

From a distance arise, the melody of dangling keys, yet still their soft chime says to them nothing, the shine in her eye, that should give it away and nothing more she should have to say and yet the intensity of that moment eludes most parents just as calmer waters bewilders seasoned sailors. "It's time," and in two simple words, a butterfly has melted butter, set hearts to flutter and made her parents think of a time when they left their homes one summer. As two friends look at each other, they know an hour has arrived when they must let fly their bird amidst the rest of her feathers.

Seconds later as a young girl slides across a door, the grass outside swivels in the wind, declaring a daring swan has in moments just past crossed a swirling river, slabs of cement revel amid a spray of water and move a little closer, a grasshopper leaps across a flower and a garage door opens slowly, his voice croaking in subdued laughter.

Soon after, as a young girl places a key in a socket, a sleeping engine awakens and reveals weeks of hunger. She eases him though her driveway with care weaving him through the streets until she reaches a highway. Here, she pushes a lever and as soon as she does, a passionate roar tells her they were always meant to be together.

Across, lurk past faces and features lost in troubled thoughts, tired and tortured, workmen and women crawl their way to home from work, harassed by the walls of the cubicles they serve, still imprisoned from the sights of an endless tomorrow. As they stare from a distance, astonished they are at the sight of a princess soaring with her lover.

Lotus

The burning rays of a rising star flirts with the skin of an angel's early hour. The heavens too laugh at a mind, which chooses to awaken along with the garden's early morning tar. "Snicker you may at the stillness of these times," says Sarah to the skies afar, "seldom is it apart from such moments that you hear clearly your hearts deepest chimes."

An offering of incense is made to the gods of peace, and she becomes on a wooden floor, the symbol of a sleeping lotus, here the quietness of thought leads her to a place where soon almost all of it shall cease. She closes her eyes and as soon as she does, pour forth a thousand thoughts from all corners of the earth. Deflecting, she focuses on a rhythmic flow, which rises and falls like the waves of a thousand still lakes.

Soon it appears a word, a chant, a wish and a door to another world. As her mantra envelops her breath, ever so softly arises the shadow of a slow but deliberate death. Soon, a voice whispers, "you may enter Sarah" and as she does, she feels she is a person no more, laying in the sands of a hazy shore, in a dreamy curl amidst a different planet's swirl.

In this paradise then does a young seeker enter, a state of being where thoughts are false but feelings true, where emotions falter and calmness pervades, where anger fades and bliss accrues, where fear disappears and pure potential appears. And yet as Sarah travels beyond borders and boundaries afar, she finds a vision as vast as the sky's she travels, buried now in the depths of her core, she aims to tame the world, rename the world, change the world and in this special moment, it appears, the hint of a deep connection, with every atom and every electron, with every photon and every phantom, with every neuron and every Saturn, with every emotion and every passion, and then arises a particular thought. Sarah! Who is she? No girl or person with that name exists, no entity with that thought persists, and in a flash, it leaves, the moment of epiphany that jolted her brain, amid a flood of ecstasy.

As Sarah slowly opens her eyes, they glow with a certain peace that radiates through her every pore, as her lids lift upwards gently, towards the shine of a lonesome star, they say, "one day, we shall drape you as well, in that moment, our innocence shall fall upon your fire and make your presence on earth too, a tale of ancient lore."

The Academy

Sarah enters through the open gates and finds herself amidst rolling hills steeped in a valley. Here, rain drops pour down steadily and birds chirp away to the tune of a sweet melody. After just a few more steps, she falls upon dazzling gardens which flow across the landscape just as Monet ravished his canvas with his favorite green.

Here, a soft hum permeates the surroundings, the dreams of Voltaire revel in the freshness of the crisp leaves, just as the writings of Dewey swell in the company of the campus trees, from the ecliptic depths of Gibran to the dizzying heights of Rumi, from the overpowering simplicity of Confucius to the opposing realities of the Tao, from the saintly murmurings of Tolstoy to the unwavering charm of Russell, from the common sense of Spinoza to the magic of Stuart Mill.

"The breeze here sings, Sarah," a voice travels to her softly, "what seems in the beginning to be meaningless chatter, turns into melodious songs a little after, soft incisions that guide and develop the birth of a flower."

"How?" asks Sarah, "with science, my love," the voice replies, "and with philosophy and with the study of the mind, of the heart and of consciousness, and of the world itself, and of the vastness of the universe and together they all come to lift a veil, a coating of the thickest paint, a curtain laid with the utmost care, a conditioning bought about with breathtaking finesse, stoked in mind and spirit as only a parent could, given a label, all packaged, in the guise of a caring caress."

"I do not understand, do you mean whatever we have learnt so far is biased? Are you saying our parents are liars?" "You misunderstand my intention, Sarah" the voice, replies, "for I have said, only, that they are admirers of tradition, a vision, that says, do and think only as us, and you shall reside in the tallest towers. The purpose of every great institution should be to remove the cloak, let the light pour into delicate veins, challenge concepts, ideas, and the literature of a thousand encyclopedias, for in an arena of learning should no subject be left untouched, no idea not discussed, and no innovative suggestion crushed, statues and replicas seemed nice in a different era, no room is there for them in ours."

"From today and for every other, impart to the world your own thinking, your own feelings and your own symphony and you shall prove, liars they all are who say, we are nothing except hostages to a predetermined destiny."

The Swan

The dying hours of each day bring about in a swan, the murmurings of a special and fascinating play, in her flight to her nest at this hour, she glides softly towards her lonely lake and slides on its surface gently, balancing her wings in rhythm with the wind, the waves gather together to welcome her home, they rush towards each other until they are on top of the other, each hoping to grace if only just a whiff of her feathers.

A journey above then must have in itself aspects of sublime magic as the swan feels the purity of air no man has and yet still he ventures in steel, so he may to himself say, I went, I saw, and I felt, if only of a little of what she does when amongst her air. They say the adventure starts truly when arriving at the pond, where with each passing second a new destiny is sworn. There are few places on this earth we live on where our senses tingle at the mere thought of its luscious lawn. The nest of a bird is where in each passing moment a new reality is born. Surely then, today must be the birth of a brand new dawn, feels Sarah as she enters a tower immersed in the shadow of a thousand trees.

A strange scent welcomes her as she glides into the warmth of its leaves, the feeling travels through her entire body until it settles into her thundering streams. Soon, tsunamis form and a thundering storm pursues until it brings forth currents of passion and desire to raise within her heart a raging fire. Strangers understand the look in her eye and return her sigh. Suddenly, he appears, an aged relic of the old war, "are you Sarah", he asks, "yes" she replies, in a drizzle only his heart can hear. How are you? His voice thunders, "great", she replies, "eager to hear the whispers of the air." Ah, he snorts, "but the weather outside is anything but fair." "This, Sir, I may not be able to bear." She replies.

Her eyes meet his and amazed he is by their fiery brilliance. The old master has seldom been so completely vanquished, his experience stretching from the beaches of Normandy to Vietnam from the Korean peninsula to the trenches in Guam, this day, taken in completely by an angel's innocent charm. Momentarily lost for words, he staggers back to reality and without another word, they move towards a caged bird of the sky.

Soon after, an ever grateful engine comes to life, inside an angel, ripples of waves form crests in her vessels and gorge them with the coming of a high as she yearns for three words from a nearby tower. "Cleared for Takeoff" a soft voice rings in her ears, and the bird roars in ecstasy freed from an earthly prison. Land rushes by faster and faster until he gently pulls back the throttle and free they are from an eternal lie. He glances towards her to verify the intoxicated high and there she is, transfixed, lost and dazzled in the breath of a delicate sigh, "is this that moment in which the world says, we too once saw an angel cry," she asks from the tear that circles her eye, "it is, young fairy," "a few words from the heart, are all I await, invisible I shall become only seconds then after."

A young girl then, looks towards the sky and shouts, "today, I feel, I too am a bird who can fly", to the earth below, she waves, "goodbye, goodbye till I die."

Dew

On a moonless night, darkness arrives along with her disguise, the shadow of her emptiness envelops the earth and shields the sky, as she drapes the endless lands she asks herself why so many of man's sins she hides. Were it not for her, would he die from guilt a thousand times each day? Or is he made so stringent and unwavering in his appetites for spoils and joys that he would continue unabated in his play?

As she chains herself to her blackness, a haze of smoke surrounds an angels stare, a nightingale glows in a neighborhood chair and the scent of a dying cigarette fills the air, the smoke soon turns into a fog and asks, for whom in this world, Sarah, do you most of all, care?" "For those", she replies, "Who suffer and still don't show their tear." "Do you mean those, who have nothing yet still have learnt to share?" "And those," she replies, "who have no hope and yet still dream to dare, truly you know as much as I, it is in our dream we live and not our eye. If realities could shriek, surely most on this earth would at once die."

The fog rises as it replies, "What you say angel is true, yet there is so little of what you and I can do", "Is that true", asks Sarah, "is this from smoke that conquered lands more vast than Mongolian hordes, enveloped oceans mightier than the greatest falls and have masked men and women as they have said their final prayer, how can you say there is nothing for us to do except wait for a lonesome tear?

One voice spoken profoundly can change into love, man's greatest fear. Did you not here of a fakir in the south, who spoke of things so different in the air, how a country he won with the strength of his dare." "You are a flower Sarah that is indeed so rare, but you talk of people who are no more here, the virus of intolerance that manifests in humanity today, no one can bear, the sickness of mayhem, war and oppression can no one shear."

"While it is true that in life, we seldom find ideas which are truly fair, at the core of our hearts sighs compassion, at every second and at every tear." "This may be true, Sarah, yet most among you are those who simply choose not to care". "Yet present there are angels in each breath of air, some, hidden below the deepest layers, others drowned in a deluge of tears, nothing exists that cannot be changed, if only we can come together and conquer our fears."

Cousins

Few bother in their chores in their days to ask, who we really are, even less are concerned in their plays to question, where on this earth did we spent our first hour. Close cousins at times then help us by reminding us of a journey from afar, guilty of treason we are when we proclaim, the distance between us and them is as much and more, than that of earth to Mars, as "nothing except a vast lie this is", scream our earth's millions of scars.

Today a father and his daughter gaze together with others at a sight which to most is as mundane and transitory as morning butter. A crowd in front of a cage gathers to delight and snigger as a fellow wanderer finds himself locked in bars of torture, the thousands who come here each day revel in the story that they are a much superior creature, together they affirm their right to imprison and jest a neighbor who bears almost entirely their own signature.

"How conscious do you feel they are?" Sarah questions her father, "I don't know", he replies, half of which is conflicted uncertainty, the other, for not wanting to enter an arena where questions haunt more than ghosts of eternity. In a cell roars an aging chimpanzee, a humble reminder of an amazing journey, through eons of years, evolving and bring about changes most extraordinary.

Sarah stares into his eyes as he does into hers. As they gaze at each other fearlessly, they peer into their histories, seeking desperately to unravel the other's mysteries. Once, not far back in the great history of the earth, they shared together a common ancestor which roamed the jungles carefree, its trees his siesta, the sunlight pouring through them his fiesta.

She born in Africa and now trespassing into different continents exploring and usurping land all over, he, simple still, the twinkle in his eye his greatest cry, hanging on to his branch in the wild, hunted and molested, his whispered protests falling on ears unaffected. The shrieks of children warn her not to stand so close to his cage, yet a flame inside burns desperately to find his story and reveal the secrets of his age.

As Sarah gazes at the sadness of his fate, a little girl of eleven musters the courage to stand along, together they move ahead of the others, but back through time. "How can it be", the younger asks the elder, "that he who is so conscious is treated as though he is not? How is it that he who feels all our emotions is greeted as though he is not? How is it that he who shares with us, the four lettered code of life, present in every mammal and every reptile, in every insect and every virus, in every dinosaur in every Cyrus matches so brilliantly and intricately with ours?

In another world he could very well have been the stalker and we the prey, would we than have had the same to say?" "If only he could talk little one," replies Sarah, "maybe the world would understand, if only he could display his feelings they would comprehend his pain, for now, he has nothing, except his jungle and his rain."

The Crush

In the roll of film, which is our life, appear a few scenes that are truly unscripted. At such moments arise clouds resembling an iron barrier erected, only a few then comprehend to make way through feelings conflicted. Sailing through an aisle at her college store is an angel awakened from her daze by a tingling in her every pore.

"Como Estas!" a Latin chord displays a melodious sound, its delicate tone hovers in the air, softly settling on Sarah's ear. "Muy Bien!" she replies softly, searching for the lips which embraced her senses and glazed through her fences. If words ever had meanings, they are lost now, if witches still practice their scheming they are history now and if simple dreaming could manifest such reeling than to the four letters of an insane feeling she must bow now.

As their gaze falls upon each other, the world around them stops and a new reality surmises, "Stay still in this moment and judge if you are to be two waves in this river," it says. As he stands transfixed, he sees in her eyes, an innocence more profound than that of the softest feather, she sees in his, the story of a life of perseverance, hope, desire and the fire of ether. Hours tick by and yet they seem like minutes, minutes fly by and they seem as seconds, seconds say goodbye and what are left are eternal moments. Students scurrying to classes, teachers preparing their trances, the world around them hurrying and flurrying past, between all this, two people stare into each other's hearts oblivious to the marches of the masses.

After what seems to be an eternity, his lips open, as he begins to search for words to convey his feelings, Sarah is already there by his side, close to him, invading his aura, questioning her own, the rush, will it stay there? Will it fly higher or will she soon tire? As he starts to speak, she guides him gently to a world outside his, where they both can become entwined together to become one forever. As Sara awaits, so do the birds, they fly no more and their feathers stall, ducks sit still in their ponds, drops of rain stop their fall and say to each other, stay still till a moment after and we shall again resemble the sky's tears.

Two smiles appear and say, together we both shall take the fall. The first steps of a delicate dance have being scripted, the outline of a fairy tale depicted, in this scene, on this set, the entrance of all intruders restricted. They walk as only early lovers could, their eyes still in sight of the other, entering a different world, a separate reality and a universe like no other.

The Princess

At times, whispers of a restful sleep remain as far from us as heavens from life's sorrow, in such moments clocks seem as if they themselves are asleep, hoping to awake in different tomorrows. In the mind flash visions by the hundreds, with the passing of each second, they come and go, yet more lingering are the passions and infractions of yet to come morrows.

"What time is it", Sarah asks from her shadow? "Three fifteen," chime the uneven hands of a slavish arrow. She returns to her thoughts, blocking some, others letting past. Suddenly it appears, the outline of an image, is it a scene? a sketch? or a dream? She asks, yet as it comes closer, it reveals the shape of a face unseen. "Who is this?" Sarah asks from her other?

Millions of neurons rush inside her brain to locate the answer, but fail to deliver, Is it the load she carries, or is it the long road that harries? She concentrates harder and millions of synapses join together to plunge deeper, soon after, they process an outlandish answer.

The face is of a girl, lonely and in tears, without a brother or a sister, father or a mother, helper or a lover, as she comes nearer, Sarah, asks from her, "angel, where lies your laughter?" "you may call me, a present day rafter," she replies, "for hundreds of years have I lived my voyage, from the straits of Gibraltar to the jungles of Africa I have seen what many have not, my story begins in the valley of Atlantis, where I was once a ravishing princess, my people more advanced than a thousand civilizations, their feats more magnificent than those of the mightiest nations."

"One day, on a boat, arrived an idea from afar, it said we were only a nation that was bizarre, that far away lived another, untainted by tar and dreamt in lust by every living czar. As the idea spread, jealousy turned to envy and became our greatest enemy, soon our paradise was overcome with insanity and my kingdom fell from grace, as the people tore and fought with each other, everything turned to rot and our heaven slid into oblivion."

"And why have so few, heard of your world?," asks Sarah, "Memories of my dazzling cities remain buried for hundreds of years, until they surfaced in the fantasies of a Greek philosopher, later in the mysteries of an American healer, and most recently in the heresies of a young seeker." "What lesson did you learn child, from the tragedy of my story?" the woman asks Sarah.

"Ideas," replies the fellow wanderer, "are fingerprints of our human signature, imprinted at times with language of our nature, at others, with the help of ancient literature. They have the power of making great, civilizations and nations, or the breaking and baking of mighty cities and stations, a day not far shall soon arise, when only those that apply to all shall remain, the rest like your island shall fall away and beg to be slain."

Clara

Friends as families arrive in different forms and designs, some easy to decipher as childhood rhymes others much harder as they traverse life in curves rather than lines. And yet there are times when one finds an entity which harbors all the different tastes of vintage wines. They call her Clara, born an orphan in a harsh winter, lived most of her days she has as a proud sinner. A free bird she is called by those who are near, a swan absurd she is named by those afar. A fiery orator she is proclaimed by those who are close, a lover of nature she is only, claims a floating rose.

They met first on a lonesome road, where one jogged and the other skipped on a rope. Entangled they became as does a moth to a flame, until they realized laughing they both were at their fall and its shame. Soon, together they leapt thinking more fun it would be if they both played the game. The same night, in the darkest hour before dawn, a beautiful friendship is cemented and sworn, as two birds lay on the beach together, they promise to cry with one eye and laugh with the other. As they both lay on the brown leather, one bares her soul to the other and says, "Protect my secrets you must, just as though they were drops of my blood in my last letter."

"Surely, I will," replies Sarah, for together we have both felt the oceans shiver." As the outline of a shining circle appears in the background, its twilight says to them, "you must live life with ease and leisure, breath each moment in a sense of wonder, think of your friendship as a divine treasure, all the while making sure you judge life with no one else's but your own measure." "We shall precious star" replies Clara, "for we are different buds, but of the same flower." Life without a true friend they say, is like a death without a witness, what of those who are alone when surrounded by the flakes of winter or those who wander aimless in search of feathers similar when a circle burns its aura on lakes, trees and a thousand leaves in summer.

The depths of love, trust and sincerity are only understood once the deepest of secrets are shared with another, when tragedies and victories both are cajoled in the arms of a sister, it is in moments such as these when scissors too break and say, "this song we can never sever, it is in nights such as these when waves from a different continent grace the feet of two grains and say "nourish these sands and others, dive into the earth and beyond her core, yet know, however far you may go, you shall be one, for now and ever.

The Kiss

Are two lovers in this world part of a plan divine? Is their sigh for each other ingrained in natures design? Is the feeling they treasure for their other, a heavenly sign? The question of profound importance at such a time becomes whether the dream leads to confine or each to dazzle like a star and shine. Sarah lays in bed as she awaits a moment laced with the purity of an unworldly ecstasy, seconds seem like minutes, minutes like hours and hours as days.

A droplet trickles down her face as the night continues her journey, the tear settles only when it settles delicately on the edge of her night gown. Suddenly, from a corner of the room, arise voices of leaves rattling and the windowsill shattering. "Is it him?" Her mind questions her heart, desperate for an answer, it starts to beat faster and faster until her senses declare, "You are in love, Sarah", in the distance leaves break, glass gives way to a flowing air and in a nearby pond, swans contend, "in the morning we shall in our flight much to say."

He appears soon after and two lovers embrace each other. As her head rests softly on his chest, his heart beat binds hers to his own and together they state, "Surely in the comfort of our sighs will the purest love arise." Ever so slowly, she arrives, a feeling, a peeling, a reeling, "who are you?" questions Sarah, "I am the high of surpassing the greatest ceiling" she replies. "I am a fog, as I am a mist, I reside within you as I live inside you, I am in your thinking, as I am in your feeling and in this moment, I am nothing except the core of your every meaning."

She looks into his eyes and they state they have much that they wish to say, in a language of intense emotion, of deep passion, and unreal elation, they carry words which reveal passages, which contain pages upon pages of three words of his true feeling. As they settle on Sarah's eyes, a hazy fog enters the room and says to them both, "Eternity is here now, in this moment, honor this dreaming as you would savor your last feeding." His lips open and place themselves on hers, time stops again, seconds, minutes, hours, all lose their allure, these are then some of the moments completely pure in our lives, at the end of it all, only about them will we be completely sure. Soon after, the wetness of their kiss merges with the clouds in the air and amid the magic that they share, together they both fly to all corners and beyond our lonely sphere.

The Angel

The world of make belief is strange, here at times women became the guardians of chivalry and men turn into stalwarts of femininity. In the last century came the realization that drama and pageantry were shades of the same symphony, for their mastery was a special place required where the ever-growing number of actors and actresses could magnify their intensity. In time this maze spread out to towns, villages and cities across the nation, where the stage assumed walls, roofs and colored halls. This Sunday, Sarah finds herself on a stage in just such a mall, where crowds swarm through the outlet stores and young boys and girls lurk the aisles for customers assuming the persona of Amsterdam whores. Lost in the chaos, she sees from afar, a woman along with a young boy, soon after, she reaches the bench and squeezes between the lady and the boy. Almost at once however, the woman asks if she may change places so she can sit beside the child. Sarah obliges amid wondering why? A closer look at the woman's face reveals a life of hardship and tragedy, another at the boy seems like staring at a sweet melody.

The goddesses of innocence must have shined on this little angel, Sarah thinks as she offers a smile to admire his innocence. He stares into her eyes, and yet he does so just for a moment, as his eyes depart almost seconds after, scanning the sea of people as does a bird envy her vast sky. As Sarah's eyes too glide through the malls various sections, suddenly stopped they are by a noise that diverts their attention, it is the voice of the boy besides her, oblivious to the world around him, his lips move in the tune of a song, it is a tune that is as profound as it is strong.

From the direction of the young boy appears a gush of sweet air, and seems to say, "Just as beautiful sceneries and magical artistries are part of a picture's reel, we too live and breathe in the same wheel." Intrigued, she looks towards the lady accompanying the boy, her face now reveals cuts and curvatures of the oceans proudest seal. Yet, what intrigues Sarah, is not the manner of the boys tone, or the style of his moan, but the words of his loan, as they are only two, and they are repeated again and again. The harsh reality of a tragic moment looms slowly, and yet when it does, so great is the impact that planets and stars that appear perfect in their trajectory now appear stationary. She searches the women's face again, and this time her eyes have changed to an expression that is both sad and blurred, the wrinkles on her forehead, confirm, "Autism", six letters of a word, and the yarn turns into the tragic story of a wingless bird.

A disability of the mind, which takes away much more than just speech and cognition. The will to live and to die join together in this concoction, served most potent to the closest, only the strongest make it across the oceans to distant shores where their joys live in the meaning of their angel's dreaming. As Sarah bends to lend the young boy her lips of understanding, furiously he recoils to the side, only to his mother will he confide, only she understands, his lonely ride. "Happy birthday, happy birthday," he sings, not bothered with the young girl who sat next to him for a day and cried.

The Ride

On the map of the United States, at the southernmost tip of its gates, a lonely road caresses the ocean waves, oblivious to earthly savagery, it lends itself only to connoisseurs of nature, who revel in its magical imagery. As two birds dazzle in its purity, fish by the millions sizzle as they attest to the picture's symmetry. Basking in joy, they sing songs of beauty, love and fantasy radiating the surrounding ocean with their symphony.

As a sheet of white clouds stretches far and wide into the cradle of this scenery, dolphins and rays too offer a glimpse of themselves and attest to the scene's serenity. Through the endless blue, love for two, takes on meanings that are completely new, amid the delicate dance of the sea, they smile at the goddesses above and say, "today we know you more than anything else we see, for we are sky birds yet never have we felt so joyous and free." In the distance, ply lumbering whales who in their songs attest, "we too agree." "Who in this world would want from such a place to flee?" ask a billion ants hugging the cement along the shore, "for there is nothing we have seen on this earth that is of an essence so pure."

"Are we in a painting Sarah?" he asks, "Verily, Jose, she replies, "For this is our hour." From afar, an eagle cries, "soon, you both shall fly away and I shall have nothing with to play, before you leave you must to these winds and oceans say, you shall come again soon as you adore our unearthly bay." They smile and say, "Only fools leave heaven, when it says, come into me and play, in the middle of our pond lays a bed we have made for you of clay, surely it is this moment only which is far more important than any day." "birds of passion you may be," exclaim the waves roaring towards the shore, "Of us, you understand nothing, come within us, so we may show you our beauty, for what you see at this moment is just the crust of our livery."

"And yet what our eyes fall upon, has within it signatures of magical artistry," the two say together, "surely we shall return to taste the essence of your liberty". "Go then!" Proclaim, the droplets of peace which roam the sea, "let your people know, there reside more emotions in each being than there are leaves on a tree, sceneries more magical than roses amid their fields, and passions that shriek louder than a slave just freed. Tell them in this world of theirs and ours, there exists a feeling of purity more vast than the southern skies, just as an oceans beauty, an oblivious world denies."

The High

Artists see the world through a lens very different. Varying shades of color do they see in each object. Vibrating pulses of light produce magic in the great cosmic fabric. They dazzle in their drizzle as they create for every poet, a new meaning in each subject.

When a painter sails in a sky full of blue, he depicts on his pallet, the beauty of an intoxicating brew. When a dancer moves relative to the rhythm of the earth, she projects in grey revelry, the fountain of her eternal youth. When a singer lends his voice to the green trees in the forest, they seek peace in the arms of his accordion chalice. When a writer walks in the middle of an ocean, the shades of green and blue fall into each other, overcome by emotion.

Sarah holds in one hand an array of varying sands amid a brush in the other, as they begin to move, they reach for the canvas and come closer together, soon, splashes of paint touch bristles of brush and they move and rub against each other. Wet with desire, they make love like lost lovers until they hear voices from within of cries of another. A thousand shades mix together in this ecstasy and a new color emerges like the birth of a flower, the trees in the distance emit a luscious scent, marking the purity of the hour and the brush sinks deeper into a new born innocence splashing the canvas with artistic fervor. It strokes the gentleness of the grass, invokes the tenderness of the clouds and cloaks the harshness of reality which stands silent without so much as a tremor.

A young girl continues to paint the world as it seems, full of beauty, artistry and tantalizing mystery. As the tiny bristles kiss passionately the surface of this picture, a blind energy flows from the new born and pastes itself firmly to the base of the caricature. In the background, a yellow star descends slowly into its restful sleep, dusk arrives accompanied by drizzle, white pearls glide on the greenery of a hillside and slide towards the scenery of overflowing flowers writhing in joy, which declare, "for these few seconds, we have spent many more in pain, severely deluded are they, who say, we are nothing but beautiful images in rain, nothing except a species in vain."

Soon an outline unfolds on a canvass in a hazy tinge of darkish blue, the first glimpse only this is she confides with a wink gracing her thigh as a droplet in the guise of a clue. As moments tick by, time shouts to her sister to light in the darkness, the spark of a gigantic fire. Space freezes, denies and then just for a second opens Sarah's eyes. The drunken dyes of soft bristles and youthful play of intricate colors magnify her cry, as she watches in stunned silence, a canvass depicting expressions of an ecstatic high.

The Plunder

The Institutional we keep chained in locked rooms and dorms, the delusional we hide in safe houses and songs and yet insanity exists in so many different forms, a variety of masks she wears at times to shield her wrongs, such is our tragedy today that our entire globe she hungrily warms. Signs and inklings persist in cities and towns, yet the masses shall do nothing until the ocean herself deforms. If the land upon which we stand does not care for us any longer, little shall we have to say to her as we never cared for her younger. As it breaks apart each day, further and further, we must realize we are refining weapons for our very own slaughter.

A time is not far when the seas shall arrive ashore, on our surprise they shall surmise, "it was a transparent dress that we for so long wore, you shall soon realize living you all were on a rented floor, little can I do now, except plunder your ore until you resemble surroundings of a millennia before." Then perhaps, a realization will dawn, listened we should have to those who begged to warn. Cast aside we did, their hankerings of old, when they said, "the earth shall implode and as slaves we shall be sold". Empty ships and planes shall then question, "Where reside our earthly inventors?" and ghost towns and offices shall moan, "Why were there only a few dissenters?"

Children young and old shall scream when they glimpse of a sky darker than the circles within their eye, "what were our ancestors thinking?" They shall ask of each other, "Did they not realize, the earth herself was sinking", a fierce lightning shall then emit from the clouds and answer, "It was self chosen blindness only that bought an end to their blinking. For as the clouds that envelop my being today, I bear witness I gave your kind, warning after warning. I told them to end their daily rape of the air, to cease the pollution of the atmosphere and not tear apart the seam of the dress the earth delicately wears. I showered them with hurricanes and storms, hoping in vain, that if nothing else, then upon watching my ire they might care, yet little difference it all made, even when we made the northern bear cry his last tear."

"What shall we do now, the children will ask, we have no home and we have no food?" "forget this dome", arrives the answer, "for it has been terribly misused." "Were our forbearers really so callous," some of them will ask? Truly it seems as if they did not for us, bother, In this at least, they should have been together." "In the end they perished just as us," a lonely bear shall shout, for our elders always said, "never would a ruling species be there for another. Now all we have left is a planet without a change in weather, a rock with nothing except an eternal summer."

The Visitor

On a velvet futon she lays, asleep in her thoughts yet awake in her heart, who could it be she asks herself when she hears her name, by the doorway stands a reclining figure, his face much older than his age, the scars on his face revealing the mind of a capricious crafter, just as the craters in his crevasses reveal shrieks of torturous laughter.

"Are you okay Sarah?" He asks, as hints of a smile accompany three curves in his face soon after. She looks at his eyes and nods, her eyes shadow her smile and together they travel in a flowing river crossing arches and gorges, logs and mighty falls and soon they land gently on overgrown grass where a tombstone stands tarnished except where a little girl once found a stone and scribbled a letter. In a few seconds only, a forgotten man in another world is amid his granddaughter once more, if only he thinks this second could become forever. Yet he leaves just as he came, in silence with a smile, the door closes and footsteps carry him away, no longer there and escaping from the injustices of a rotating sphere, how wonderful she feels, that he too has sensed the calm and the peace, as for just a moment he saw from a window the world that she sees.

Words don't seem necessary when distant worlds appear the same, where fairies and goblins too have a name, where such a word as shame has no fame. Where other peoples and societies are never to blame, where nations and countries are never sought to tame, where life is infinitely more sacred than a soldiers game. At times reality merges into fantasy and the meaning of life's subtle symbols become hard to decipher, it is in moments as these that purpose in life is what must always one remember. Where the heart may falter the mind must stop her, where the mind may alter the heart must hold her.

It is amid such transitory eclipses that one seeks the treasures of a land afar, from the currents of these torments people learn who they really are. Birds across the land and the sky talk to their feathers through the expression of their sigh. Our feelings speak for us, almost all of the time, why do they not then for the other, chime?

The Gallery

There are some on this earth, who can observe with one sense much more than those with all five, in deep sadness do they traverse the world in which they see soul's dead even when they are alive. Together they breathe the scent of an obscure gallery, where ancient elements in the air softly slither away their sanity. Brushes of paint signify damsels lying on a silky grass, cut in a thousand pieces they are by thundering sermons of a weekly mass. Another screams of innocent children shredded from family and country, loaded on ships for another continent and asked to become slaves of a nation afar.

"Surely this must only be fictitious art," exclaims Jose, not realizing it was caricatures as these that inspired a revolution to start. The next talks of torture, men hung from the gallows by the hundreds, vivid illustrations of another evolution. A third invites the psychotic to indulge in their fantasies with rigor and lust, an image of rape and plunder amid a fire, women lie with their pregnant stomachs slit, their unborn babies on the tip of their enemy's sword, the stink of hate tied to their tarnished cords.

"This is crazy Sarah, why are we here?" questions Jose, this is reality my flower, of an illusion that does not care, that forever continues to shear and never appears to spare," she replies. They say in the strange and senseless do we peel away our insanity, face to face with our pretentious vanity, it seeks to destroy a certain sense of self only to impose yet another, which comes with its twin, a daze at a far slower pace, flirting like a striking vase, dazzling us till eternity amid a mesmerizing maze. In simple form, three paintings show the true debasement of man's nature, at times with a signature from obscure scripture, at others with witnesses from ancient literature, together they have kindled fires, shattered hopes and battered a million souls. All reminders to us that we act and play even today in the same continuing picture.

Strokes of a brush then show more to us then what we can fathom, only when we are in them and feel their every tear do we then learn a little something about the air we all share. Jose settles his hand into Sarah's, his mind wandering trying to make sense of it all, she pressing her essence into his, lost in the wilderness of her grief, wondering what she must do to stop the horror of the web our earth weaves. "Take with you, this message," she says to the wind, "to every corner of our lonesome sphere, come together we must, putting aside our simple jealousies, petty rivalries and differences in our allegories, grace each other as fellow wanderers we must, to create the serenest symphonies."

Sin

In the deep hours of a moonless night, thirsty glances of a monstrous wave crash into open sands satisfying only momentarily, a ravenous hunger. Soon after, her ripples of desire follow young boys and girls to the edge of a raging bonfire.

The dark sky above dazzles with billions of dancing stars, hiding and sliding one from the other, each trying in vain to outdo the other. "Should we sever this night of December?" asks a daughter from her mother. "Wait a while longer, says her elder, for we shall begin our plunder only when they are all together." "Shall we truly peel away their fire by the push of a lever?" the wave asks again from her shelter," "We shall surely, for we too inhabit their nature," shouts the reply.

Strange clouds then in the horizon appear and say, "Do not caste even a glimmer of an eye towards innocent feathers, for in seconds I shall scream and cast upon you, a million curses of an eternal thunder, what shall be left of you then shall only be a tears of bewildering wonder. Stay calm and inside your homes and I may save you this night from a horrific plunder."

"On a lonesome beach at a distance much further, two lovers revel in the breath of each other, their hearts sway in the beat of their song and in the hours that patiently linger, they state tonight and for every other, we are one forever." On this night of ecstasy, some will dance as others will sing, only a few will lay upon the other and say we are one and we sin.

As the ocean swells in anger, it says, "lover's you may be, yet many rules you break in your daring incursions, slayed you all I would have, were it not for the hovering clouds and their inflamed emotions", "Where if not here, grains of sands ask of waves mighty? Would you rather that we not live our humanity? Is this the sum of your theology of piety? Surely, when you were young, you loved your freedom, then the whole world was your kingdom and your hesitation was seldom. Hypocrisies and tyrannies rule our day, when standards different are in every house hold at play. Do the birds not fly high with their wings spread across the sky. Why should young lovers then hide behind earthly shutters to cry? If there is a sight in this world in which almost everything that has meaning would at once die, then surely it must be the tear in a lover's eye". "We accept then, our surrender," say millions of waves as they forsake the night's agenda, "Never did we ever imagine sin to be so innocent a feather."

The Voyagers

Some time ago, European voyagers chanced upon a strange and exotic space of land, where lived ancient Indians who toiled in its breathtaking beauty with nothing other than their spirit and their hand. The travelers bought with them stories and allegories of millions who sinned and were damned. In time, the fear spread and became the ore of a fantasy that became grand. Amid massacres and tortures they became conquerors who spread the flames of a fire across the sand and a fairy from afar wept, as her delicate fingers struggled to reach for her magic wand.

Yet a few hundred years after, the madness of an ancient world cried herself to sleep, blinded by the glare of new knowledge and wisdom, an advent in our history that is surely the greatest leap. How is it then that after a few hundred more we live in a world where much of same seeps? "Is this why the fairy still weeps Sarah," asks another, decades younger. "Time for bed angelic droplet of a heavenly shower" orders Sarah, "For if you sleep now, you just might in your dreams see yourself flying above the tallest tower." "Only if in my dreams there are people who shout, "we seek laughter over power," and then whisper, "much better will this world become soon just wait for a little while after."

Sarah smiles at the shine of innocent plaster and murmurs, "at such young an age, and already a natural rafter!" "What happened to the Indians then Sarah? Did they survive in their pavilions or did they sigh their last in their millions", continue two curious eyes at an unusual hour. "Devastated they were in that day and age, assimilated they are today in play in another cage. Only a few now remain, eager to join the race for a meager wage. Their story died soon after, when their elders chose to continue their homage to an ancient sage, neglect they did to adapt to a modern world, for had they done so their destiny would have spoken of an infinitely different page."

"And the voyagers from afar? What became of their fate?", "They embraced technology and kept alive within them, the restless flame for modernity. With wisdom, hope and persistence did a few among them rise above the rest and nourished their burgeoning cities with the most amazing tapestries. A while after they dazzled the rest of the world with the most amazing document in living history and said to the world come unto us, dwell and reside forever within the solitude of our United States."

Feelings

"What is a feeling Sarah? Do we even know if she is to us, true? How is it that since the dawn of time, she has poured on us her morning dew, yet of her birth her aims or dreams we have not a clue." "Because she blossoms in her purity only within a few, while the rest stand deluded by a scenic view, no picture in this world or any other remains static, change it must Jose, just as the sky allows the cloud to hide for a time, his lonesome blue." "But is it not the case Sarah, that her essence we cannot configure, her presence we cannot deliver, her lessons we do not remember and only her fragrance it is that we can treasure."

"The depth of her soul Jose, asks that we sail away from oceans of words and into lakes of emotions, where, fairies await mixing their brew." "I understand from these words nothing Sarah, for I see no fairies, as I hear no whispers, all I ask is to understand the design of an elusive crafter". "If you look at me closely Jose, you shall see in my two eyes, the curiosity of flexible plaster, yet if you stare at me for a few minutes more, you shall begin to feel within your heart, songs of your happiness and laughter.

"Soon after you shall travel to a place where lions will cry and little girls will growl, where cats will bark and dogs will purr, where the leaves will talk and the grass will fall, where shadows will shout and the sun shall whisper and it shall be spoken and stated, I am she who you seek in earthly dwellings, know this, I reside only in your heart where I breathe only when I am elated." "Verily, Sarah, I can see now, the outlines of your whisper, for it was feeling only that was present when we were nothing, snatched we were from eternity to be bought upon this space where many still suffer in infamy." "Is it her fear then, that propels humanity into the well of make belief certainty, is it she who proclaims loudly her naked bigotry, could she really be the reason for our insanity?" "Yes Jose, for her net spans each entity and yet why fear who we have known since the beginning of time, after all it is only recently that we have adopted a body" and placed into it our present reality", replies Sarah.

You're right and you are high!" "Am I?" She questions as she looks at the exploding stars that crisscross the sky, "Let us fly then, Jose," she says, as her hand moves across his eyes, here they proceed to gently shut its doors, her fingers slide downwards and across his face, where they weave across the rough edges of his skin and press against the growth of his hair and feel that must soon stop, alas they might make something in him tear. "Feel deeply each caress Jose, for similar it is to the sun, which burns daily to impress his shadow, understand your passions and treasure your feelings, even if they resemble flights of a dying sparrow, for no one truly knows if there shall even be a tomorrow."

Lust

Amid the early seconds of dawn, just as the sun begins to break free from his cage, a mountain feels that he has begun to age and a young seeker finds herself in search of a renowned sage. As she traverses his lonely pasture, unaware she is of his thirst to hold and capture. She looks for a path shorter than the others, one which would take her further and much higher all other's.

The giant hill holds her in his gaze and says to the clouds, "an eternity it has been since one such as this has crawled upon my skin, I beseech you today, for you shall not bother me if I sin." "Never have we ever so callous been," reply the clouds, as they gather to watch a spectacle they have since years not seen.

As she trudges a broken and rustic path, she feels the trees murmur as they sway, further along are grasshoppers and butterflies who whisper to each other as they play, but the strangest of all is the grass by the side of the lake, which positions itself dreamily basking in the suns ray. Tired, she drops to the floor where the grass brushes away her tears and asks her not to cry, he helps her to stretch her legs and cajoles her to look at the sky, then gently closes her eyes and asks her to feel the high. As shutters slide across her eye, she feels pricked and pierced over and across the length of her thigh. The grass grows in size and she feels in her ear, the sounds of ecstatic sighs. The ground beneath begins to shake violently as the mountain screams his cries, he intensifies his rise and soon arrive millions of sensations exploding in thunder amid an angel's half shut eyes.

"Earthling", he calls out to her a little after, "I beg you to forgive this ailing sinner for his transgression, for I have days left on this land very few, were it not for my centuries of frustrations, I would never have planted in you in this incision." Dazed, she questions, "Was it you then, who took me in his arms and flew me across to distant galaxies and their stars?" who allowed me pleasures deeper than the tunnels on mars? Who made me forget a life based on minutes and hours? "Yes", he replies, "it is I who made you smell the nectar of newborn flowers." "What is your name, then", he asks. "It is Sarah", a soft voice replies, "Fallen deeply I have in your

48

charms young flower, will you not make me your one and true lover?" "Even if I could precious hill, how long shall last your sacred lava, for love is infinitely more deeper than an orgasmic hour, soon it might be that another will saunter along, and in me you shall lose all interest and desire."

"Never Sarah have I of anything other been such a great admirer, for I have touched you in places and spaces which host your most raging fires and yet you gift me wisdom which has long since expired." "Searched I have the world over for my sire and savior, yet found nothing I have except a path to the graveyard." And realized today I have dear hill, how empty it is, this search for seers and sires, life is much too short to roam around another's towers, one must look within only and soon shall appear, a path amid its showers."

Magic Kingdom

Sarah fly's towards the edge of a town where magic is brewed in the guise of a mouse. Amid the luscious layers of a blue sea she circles his kingdom hoping to glimpse a sight of him before the night falls and blinds her wisdom. Millions gather at his door each day to say, "Once, we too saw him play." They throng the castle's vast gardens and grounds, enthralled in each minute by as many clowns.

As she maneuvers her companion to steal a closer look at the vast pavilions, breathless she becomes when her eyes spot a familiar figure, welcoming the crowds and wearing his medallions. She opens several beads from the face of her brown bag and removes from within, a silvery piece of metal. She aims it his throat yet is unable to fire, for in her haste to capture his fiefdom, her stallion rocks his wings amid the clouds and shrieks, "never, in this moment shall I allow you the taste of this desire and if you persist, the consequences for you shall be most dire." "Why?" She asks, as she grabs his throat and orders him to kneel. He struggles to break free and complains to the roaring winds. Amongst themselves, they quietly conspire and call on him to float gently into their bellies and snuggle within their billowing sins. His speed falters, as he climbs into the heights of thunderous gusts, higher and higher until suddenly thrown from this tremendous height he is with a force, which whispers, "Have you never realized, for it is in our hearts to lie."

Falling akin to a penny from the vastness of the sky, cradled back to safety he is by Sarah, who returns once more to traumatize him in this game of mystery. She touches him softly gracing his reins with her fingers until he circles cautiously, yet only moments pass by and he glimpses a shadow of silver in her hands. He screams, "not here" and breaks loose from her grip until he floats gently towards the edge of a cemetery. Sarah shouts that if he does not obey, she will keep him in his cage and throw his keys to a monstrous handler. He declares then, as he never has before, "Wait just a little while longer, trust today in me and your faith shall forever be stronger." She feels in his passion, tears of sincerity and let's go of the yoke thinking of his frailty.

The engine roars as it moves towards the playground of fantasy where even the dying open their eyes to live for a short while in a new and different reality. Soon the scene appears again, nestled in the midst of green vegetation, the dazzling tapestry of a mouse's castle, ever so gently he lowers his speed and arranges his height just so that Sarah has from her window at this very moment, the most amazing sight. The engine's hum declines into a course and husky whisper, it points to the silver in her hand and says, I shall no more wither, you may open now the curtains of her shutter and snap in this moment the perfect picture."

The Aquarium

Fish locked inside a box are similar to birds concealed in a cage, their inhabitant stolen from them at an early age, jailed they are in a lonely cell, sealed forever at a measly wage. Yearn they must every hour of the day, for one glance at their past in a shallow bay. As they travel every second, the breath of their small world, envy they do every moment, the life of an ocean ray.

As they pass each day in an eternal prison, they beg to say, "For a little while only, let us dance in the open sea so we may merrily sway." What difference between her and a slave of today, both for our amusement, jest and horrid play, justify ourselves as we may try, our actions betray whatever we may say. Such is the condition that millions toil in day to day, yet all we offer them is "work hard and continue to pray."

On a bedside table, the beat of a clock fastens as she asks, "Why for the poorest, can we not make debt a pardon?" A singer of acclaim sings through his poster and says, "at least in Africa, I tried through my fame". Bubbles of water shout from inside a glass, "Spread far and wide you must, the incense of this flame". A lamp in a corner flickers, "Is it not a shame that we continue to blame ourselves, when we must ask, what is to be our aim?" Amid the wail of this cry arises the haunt of a tragic lie. The eagle of a coin turns to laughter and says to them all; "desires of my own, I must only look after, they who cry shall die and keep forever asking why, for what I earn is surely only my." The clock erases all concept of time as the lamp bursts into the light of the sun.

A shade of steam envelops the water and she boils until she can control herself no longer. "Your corporate mafia's and imperial powers in their tireless attempts to increase their ocean of dowers leave in their wake, only shallow lakes full of poverty stricken laborers. When war and profit become one and the same, than death and misery become just another game. Do you not realize in your lust and aim, generations of hope you forever maim?"

"Do not despair", arises the voice of a forgotten curtain, for it is true that I am almost always bound, yet there are times when my arms are opened and in these moments I feel from a distance the breath of a different air. For together tears can form oceans of care. Overcome your fears and transcend you shall the heavens mightiest layers, only then shall you release the fish from her plea and let her swim free in her sea.

The Touch

They sit at each other's side as they swivel their feet in the rushing tides of the water. Colors fall into each other as the sun bakes them over and over, from a violet yellow to the whiteness of the lake's shadow, richer, purer and surer of their alluring beauty, it is this serenity which makes wings of the sky bird's flutter and the twigs of the mulberry trees to stutter. "What do you make of love, Jose?" A question that has so many answers is disguised by the symmetry of the most innocent of eyes. He stares into them as they do into him and to each other they say, "We must go deeper for the answer." "If you place in my hand one of yours and close for a moment all senses except one, a beat of your heart shall connect with the breath of a flower and you will feel in our embrace, the high of flying from the tallest tower." Sarah, places her hand in his and imagines herself in the cradle of a thousand clouds being lifted up all the way into heavens unknown until she reaches a plateau where fairies are angry, but the gods are happy, where fire is wet, but the water is burnt, where the selfish are proud and the caring are thrown to the ground, where the guitar is singing and the singers are humming.

She continues to climb higher and higher until a whisper speaks into her ear, "Do you see a reality which makes no sense Sarah, so different and insane that it makes every bone in your body shudder with fear. This is an emotion Sarah, which stems from a feeling, which blossomed from a thought, which was seeded by an angel who came in quietly and planted it in your desire, she is the wire through which the current of your energy flows, the invisible force through whom your destiny glows, the slayer of a barrier who long ago proclaimed, the gates of pride, ego and selfishness are forever closed." "But I have no fear", she replies, the wind cajoles the air as they configure an answer, they breeze through the park until they arrive together to lift her hair. "Go higher Sarah," a whisper of passion states and as she holds tightly his hand once more, it begins again, the flight to a vast and uniquely different shore.

As Sarah fly's into space, she sees in the distance, lights by the millions, as they begin to brighten, a wave of ecstasy envelops her body, in every pore and every ore she feels the glow of shimmering synergy. As the high takes over the breath of her heart, a gentle whisper emanates from the winds draft, "Four letters of a word Sarah mean nothing just as the cut to the finger is a little more than a tingling, feel only the beat of his heart in the warmth of your hand and you shall know what you feel in the soft flow of your sighing."

The Titans

In the beginning, there was only philosophy, an Ionian venture into mystical novelty, it remained for centuries the handsome stature of an ancient world's poverty. While the rest of the world languished in bloodshed and ignorance, a few gods in southern Europe basked in the radiance of an unholy brilliance. They sought to explain the nature of our universe and fought to train a river of youth, dangers of the oracles curse. They came and conquered for centuries after, with stories and allegories, myths and legends, apologies and mythologies and for an eternity in antiquity, reigned supreme in knowledge of the divine hereafter.

"Michelle", interrupts Steve, "a lover of wisdom, that you are, you must confess, they asked questions with no answers, they had rulers with no numbers, were they not just stage singers with no dancers?" "Surely, you jest", she replies, "the fountains they fermented, for years after cemented the wisdom of the skies in its layers and the knowledge of a thousand arts in all spheres.", "only amid a million tears, Michelle," announces Clara, "for soon, it turned to dust in the sky when theology arrived and thrust upon the world, her showers of answers. She ruled supreme across continents and oceans, her empire stretching from the shores of Ireland to the gates of china. Her iron rule encompassed all, it made cities and nations with its heartbeat fall and made her Rome, the strongest of all. As a stream of prose, in its various forms arose, it spread across and covered the barren petals of an ancient rose".

"And Yet this is hardly the end of the story," says Sarah, "After running her course through antiquity, philosophy did cry all the way to the cemetery and yet before her goodbye, she baked with her bare hands, a clay of arrangement and measurement which paved for the late arrival of the story of science. The new art then stole from theology, nearly all of her glory and showed inhabitants of this world, tantalizing new beauty. With method, sense and purpose did she arise, awakening slowly from her dark slumber and along with her arose, true titans of their fields, one after the other, Keppler and Copernicus, Galileo and Newton, Espinoza and Bacon, Darwin and

Spencer, Faraday and Einstein, and many more who bought sanity to an outdated world, who sought answers to all and bought with them, a light for those to hold who in their darkness had for centuries surmised, since we are born, we are headed towards an eternal fall."

The Neighbor

"You have a lovely garden, Ms. Bradshaw," a girl says to another much older. "Yes it is Sarah, but is my grass beautiful or the two pearls that gaze at it?" "Whatever do you mean?" She asks her elder, "When I was young like you I was told to cherish sceneries which hold my fancy, after only a few years of wandering I discovered I roamed in empty pastures neglecting my own beauty." "I do not understand," replies Sarah, "You shall soon", she says as she fills her vase.

Sarah searches for clues to the puzzle laid before her yet soon after forgets the musings of an aging dreamer and her eyes settle on a small flower, battered by yesterday's ferocious wind, she dangles hopelessly in a neglected corner. Even in this state her beauty radiates a spectacular aurora, amid this, a leaf on a nearby tree wishes he had been a better lover.

"Are you in love," the spinster asks, looking directly into Sarah's eyes. A second passes before her lips part, but they need not have, her eyes had already given away the answer. "Tell me Sarah, how do you feel when you are in his arms? Unsure of how much to say, she smiles, "Of course," the old lady says, and "what about when he plants his lips across yours?", "My mind tells me I am in this world, but my heart promises I am in another", replies Sarah. "And do you miss him when he is not near?" she asks again, "I do," replies an intrigued Sarah. "Tell me, what do you think happens to lovers who have never felt their others caress? Who have never had the courage to confess? Who have never ever felt what it is like to feel the wetness of a kiss?' "I cannot say," she replies, "Did you not wonder when you saw my dying flower how she loved him but never said a word, how she wanted to hold him when her sisters told her it was a thought absurd, how she dreamt of a drop of rain, flowing from him to her through a flying bird? Have you never thought of love and felt, she is in all places and spaces, sung and heard? "Did you never think of a neighbor who danced with her angel in lakes and rivers only to awaken and find herself in a desert?"

At times, an unusual stillness is all that is required for remarkable things to happen, a few seconds pass and soon after a girl walks into a garden. A hysterical leaf is then cut from her root and placed upon a decaying flower, as Sarah stares at them both, she says, a thought arrived moments ago and said, "Sarah, you float on the surface of what an emotion should be, for a little while only, let an entity free, which screams night and day, if only for a few seconds, let my love be with me."

Adi Khan

The Assignment

"Have you ever looked at a fan, have you ever seen the mist that develops between its blades, considered how its fog evolves into a cloud and twists round and round, over and over, in one motion, spraying the air forward with an unnatural uniformity amid an untold devotion. Have you ever felt while feeling the presence of this air that sometimes in our lives we face more than we can bear? Have you ever felt that your pinnacle is from you not far, just that one break and you would become forever, a shining star? Have you ever dwelt on that final moment of insanity, which lies always not ashore, but remains within reach, always hugging our core? Does it disturb you that just as the blades of the fan cut into a million pieces those thin slices of air, our hatreds and our fears are just such spades slicing a thousand others, but most fiercely our own fates.

Why then, must our country be better than the other, our society fitter then the other, our people saner then the others, our wisdom higher than the other. Is it fair to say that you are greater than the other, as you were born in one nation and not another? Is it sane to walk our path blind, to follow an ideology of hate, jealousy and hypocrisy, a legacy that pities brother against sister, and father against mother. With myths and allegories does it rule over the masses, in vast establishments of order, where hate is taught amid fiery speeches in thick marshes of grass, where guns fire and burn in youthful souls the thirst of a murderous desire.

From the history of our world, important lessons must be learnt, respect and obedience without critical thought must never be earned. The fan shall blow until extinguished at its source. Its power, arising from the deep slumber of the majority, who even asleep are devoutly afraid of it's over powering authority. Let us become rebels then, to nationalistic fervor, to unjust wars of power, to patriotic pride, let us stem the rising tide and choose our own path and its ride. Let us turn to humanity and peel her skin so we may seek her glory, for there is so much more in common among us than that apart. A shower then do we require at this hour, only she can remove the toxins in the atmosphere and bring forth a thundering gush of cool air. May we all be so lucky to hear her breath some day." As Sarah walks back to her seat from in front of her class, an eerie silence enters the room intent on creating an emphatic plunder. She remains just for a few moments, as she is blown away soon after, scared from an ovation that reminds her of a recent thunder.

Fear

Sarah struggles with the yoke as screams of angry clouds tear across the fabric of the skies. Darker and darker they become, shouting, "Come forever within us and dwell, or we shall crush thee and sip from your innocence, the froth of heavenly rum."

In a state of distress the world becomes narrow, it assumes the persona of a stalking shadow and exhumes from nature the delusions of a taller tomorrow. In such times, the minutia hairs on the edge of the skin tend to grow, in the veins, floods of hormones gather like the flakes of early snow, like the queen of the Niagara and amid a thunder, they start to row, in the deep crevasses of a sponge, legions of soldiers take a vow and then rush to battle, with their armor in the symmetry of an extravagant flow.

Vanity must be shattered, sanity must be cajoled and mountains of bravery must form and take hold. Belief in ability must surmount the faith in destiny, the presence of an inner force must overtake the insistence of nature's resource and the will to conquer fear must be stronger than the shear of the greatest slayer. In moments such as these, young girls often search desperately for their shining knights who arrive amidst blinding lights, snatch them from the jaws of thunder and fly them to their castles on the wings of their magical kites. Yet, this day, no sign there is of a handsome savior, nothing can she hear around her except the whisper of a final barrier. From nowhere, suddenly she appears, a scream from deep within, it holds her in its grip and tightens its grasp, until it charms her with its grin, "Never, Sarah,", it says, "can we ever, surrender."

And these are the moments when the most decisive decisions in one's life are made, in the passing of just a few seconds are all weapons thrown to the ground and laid, or a will to fight, persist and survive is declared. Inside the soft layers of her skin now rage floods and tsunamis, on every shore and in every pore, a force develops that surpasses the strength of the purest ore. With vigor and passion she guides her craft through rain and lightning until reason and purpose she sees in the core of each draft. Struggling to win over the rampaging winds, she talks with men and women, who sit high inside a tower, scared they are for her as they berate the lair of this horrendous air.

Eternity, it seems arrives before she was summoned, when suddenly a flirtatious cloud glances, smiles and amid his open arms, cries, "if you wish, angel you may enter, for my shadow shall help you reach your river." "Gracious I shall remain forever to your ardent desire," she replies, for your shadow however, my wings shall forever flutter." Soon after, cradled in the scent of his shower, she is lowered to the land by the shores of flowing water.

As the rubber of her plane's tires burn the runway and the soft drizzle mixes with the sweat of friction, Sarah looks up and thanks again, heartbroken feathers of a lovers sigh, as he says goodbye he winks and says, "look within, Sarah" and as she does, she glimpses just for a moment, the dance of her essence where fear has just died.

Bliss

In disguise he appears, with greetings wrapped in a shawl of mist. "Today", he says, "I shall take you to a land of eternal peace. This place I speak of, she is truth and desire, to feel her scent, millions would go through the hottest fire." Sarah lifts her eyes to those of Jose, they face each other and soon, each flutter lifts and says, "We must leave now, for after this, there is nothing else to utter".

He motions to the sun and she burns a little brighter, the sky in the distance follows, and stands a little taller. The clouds break their embrace, away they must now falter. He lifts them both and slides them into a boat, it speeds across layers of glistening ocean, and in the middle of nothing stops and drops all of its anchors.

Now he says, they must taste the essence of a mighty ocean. Tanks filled with the air of life are saddled on shoulders and soon they are pushed to live among natures underground soldiers. The eyes have a distinction of seeing all things beautiful, yet even they are stunned into silence at the removal of an earthly wool. Life shines in amazing complexity in the depths of an endless sea, her sights seem divine as they both together swear such beauty they might never elsewhere see. Fish of all stripes roam the forest and the trees, dolphins laugh and play in the calm of the blue seas.

All around them is a universe which sings to them its own magical verse. A few minutes after, he says "for now, this is all that I can offer." As they arise from the sea, he cajoles the water and she breathes for them her petals, showering them with tears of salty powder. "This," she says, "You may save so your heart may each day beat a little louder." "Must we go back", Sarah pleads, "only if you promise to forever look after", he replies and in his sighs, tells them the story of how man came, saw, and took from the blue ocean, the purity of her laughter." Soon on land they arrive and as they glance at each other, together they say, "We may on this clay, survive for another day, yet moments ago in a giant's belly alone were we alive, amid sceneries and serenities a thousand times softer."

The Actor

With half the class sleeping and the other half dreaming, the professor continues to rant unruffled at the boredom pervading across the hall, he continues his act on stage convinced that beneath the rugged exterior of his cynics, there reside in the audience waves upon waves of silent admirers. Such is his love for his stage that he would perform for empty chairs, such is his passion for his art that he would rather die than see his canvass without a stain. Each day across the many layers of our world are plays such as this enacted, in which a teacher is little more than an aspiring actor, while the world showers him with pity, little do they realize, lost he is in ecstasy as he is of his plays both producer and director. Most ignore his eccentric ways as they imagine knocked to the side of the road he was in his own day, if only they knew, each moment of his life he floats in the sky as he lives daily his scripted plays.

Just as the last eleven days, today a young girl slides further into her chair, soon after, two tentacles of soft whispers lodge themselves in her ears and she orders her eyes to focus on his hands only instead of his stares. Only a few moments have gone past when she feels lost she is completely, in the charms of his arms floating in heavens listening to the merriest songs.

A strange thing it is then, listening to art when we turn of its sound, how many can claim that they can understand without a voice, an entity without a crown? How many have followed the ascent of fingers as they slowly lift themselves towards the sky and speak of her wonders? How many have studied palms as their sweat talks of the poor man's struggles? How many ponder on delicate veins when they speak of the greatest lakes and rivers? How many stare at nails when they point towards the oceans and reflect her layers? How many watch bristles of hair, when in their sway they sing about the sky and her stairs? How many gaze at the curves of skin when they talk about their earth and cry her tears? Perhaps, to greater depths we must fall before we see art in such forms, maybe further in the forests we must travel before sentences without words can make us see our wrongs.

The Stare

His face was pale, shallow and hollow, dimples and crevasses in his sunken cheeks tried to bring to it something of a scenery but so often as they do, they failed in their attempts to present a pleasant view. Instead a battered and tired existence came to the fore, which spoke of arduous hours spent gazing outside of a bedroom window yearning for the dreams of his younger years. If one looked carefully enough, it screamed for the first few moments just after he had glimpsed the sight of his only love.

As I stood by watching him gaze up at the sky, left wondering I was about the thoughts that were stalking his mind, for I could have sworn an hour had passed since I first saw his eyes, transfixed at one spot not stopping to ask why. Just then a voice crackled in the distance, I turned at once to see if he had flinched, only to realize while my mind had raced to his bench, my head had wanted to look for the crow, soon came a cold and silent breeze, as it entered my brain, she said of his intentions, impressions or obsessions I would never know. How I asked her, could he stare at one place without so much as a whimper, how if he could do this, was he not in life a winner?

And what is your definition Sarah she asked, of this word you so admire? I replied that I felt that he was dead, even though he was still alive, in mourning even though he had survived and in a cast even if he had been a prince in his past. Have many, she asked, have beaten life at her game and said, ready we are for our prize, never ever has an entity been honest when it has said, with life we battled and soon after were declared the victor. Whatever do you mean? I asked her again.

A whistle blew and the leaves started moving, as branches began to sway, a few fell, as they yelled, "we find your questions, profoundly amusing". "Even the youngest among your species would know, there is only one winner and she isn't you, even a snail would say soon, I shall see myself covered in grey, no matter how hard I pray, even slumbering trees can predict victories when men and women are without a clue, even a whale would say, there is only a certain time for my stay." And yet if what you say is true, why does he stare at one place and not two? I ask again, "because, where he goes he has no need", they together reply, "in the end, all a man asks of himself is whether the road was black or green, what matters then is not if he has won, but only how the journey has been.

The Marsh

From above the troposphere and nearly into regions of outer space, pictures have been assembled of a lump of sugar protruding from the belly of a Giant. These snaps show in exquisite imagery, the topography of a heavenly symmetry surrounded by a deep blue ocean, flat and even, its tapestry basking in a glowing charisma, exuding in its sunlit lawns, a pink flamingos poetry. In its center, resides the echo of a tremendous crater covered all around by the scent of water, she is today the source of all its power. She hides in her bosom thousands of secrets, some told, others buried forever. The stage of a hundred battles, she carries with her the perfume of ancient Indian sages, her history alone, mesmerizing the present with its army of pages. By the thousands they look towards her for an escape from monotony, she smiles in return and says, "At your own risk, you may."

Today, Sarah and her friends bask in its murkiness, sliding deep into one of its alleys with a boat not much larger than an ocean ray, they lazily follow the breadth of its shallows, singing and laughing, when suddenly bubbles of water appear amid dark shadows. Danger is a vague word, as it surrounds us often but then leaves soon after, Death is more familiar but only because it envelops others, leaving us only to ponder. In truth both, even to themselves are a stranger, as unaware they are of life and the strength of her wager. There are however, a few moments when one feels a prickling, a sensation that is more ghastly than both combined, she is called fear and she arrives truly when one is faced with imminent slaughter. How does one then describe the teeth of an Alligator? How does one in such moments find any or even one word or letter? Is it even possible to remain alive when shrouded by the cloak of a savage murderer? The three friends stare at the descendent of a mighty mammal, his jaws open and wet with excitement, his paws slowly snaking their way towards a boat at the end of a river.

Screams ring out in the trees and the air as they struggle to paddle away from his murderous lair. They thrust their oars wildly in the water, and make war with her over and over, yet progress in this endeavor they make no further. His eyes lust at the sight they see; Three humans mixed with salt and water and he shall be full till a week after. He narrows the gap stealthily, as the waves make way for their giant monster. Just a few moments left in this strange adventure, and yet as life often does, she brings into this picture the songs of her saviors. As the sounds of their screams travel beyond the marshy water, soon several boats arrive and spray the giant beast in their midst while their inhabitants state "surely you all are too young for the hereafter."

Pores

In love with you Sarah I was since the first time my skin caressed yours, in touch with your every breath I became when my toes became warm in your pores. My emotions exploded first when fall appeared and took from you your clothes, yet how shall I ever explain to you the feelings which arose when my feathers said you are so much more than your naked prose. Day after day as I feel your heart beat flow, a voice from inside myself says, I want more and more and yet when I see others staring at your ore, I feel a pinch that cries, "Only you should be by her shore".

There were times early on when I thought the storms would destroy our dome, if only I had realized our nest rested on a wooden foam. How can I ever forget how during perennial rains your outstretched hands made for us a shelter and we felt truly that we lived in a home, where would I be at this moment if I didn't have you in my arms, when so easily we could all have been torn. Who would have thought amidst each other's shoulders and arms we will have grown. Who would have guessed your slightest moan could make a tree's root freeze, how many would believe today that your smile can make the wind cease. Every second, of every minute of every hour shows, you feel as much love for me as the ice at the poles did when she for her bears froze.

Who would have surmised, cousins which drifted apart over millions of years, would one day say to the other, "so different we are, and yet so close." And never Jose, did I ever feel that I was in the company of those I did not adore, as the first time my arms laid their eyes upon your glide, they said, never have we ever seen, such an entity before, as soon as you graced past my leaves, tiny fissures appeared to say "never have we gazed at an innocence so pure." As your friends scurried to build a nest for your stay, little did they know I had already arranged a thousand toys for your play, as they flew across the meadows to look for food, how would they have known, their Jose had already cooed.

Together we have felt life laughing when we sung her first song, smiling when you fell across the lawn and sighing when you watched my legs feel the air between them at dawn. One day while you were playing with my curls, a gust of wind arrived and gazed at your hand, she stayed for a while without uttering a word, until she could bear it no longer, and said "this picture should never be torn."

The Sigh

"What shall happen to us when we die professor?" A mermaid asks a fellow wanderer, "can I write today to the world, my final letter, or is it too early yet to embrace an eternal winter?" "Strange Sarah that such thoughts should roam your mind, unheard of they are in young girls of your kind." "But does not suppression give way to rebellion, professor, why must we be so scared of reflecting on the end of our time, for it may be that what we fear most could be a pasture, sublime."

"Explain further what you mean Sarah, for your words hasten me to cliffs where hard it might be for me to in this age climb." "The other day sir, I watched an insect child cry, as her parents were slaughtered by a shoe's ignorant glide. Alone in torment I watched her suffer as she wandered about our earth searching for shelter, from village to village she roamed, yet no one would stop to help her, until finally her eyes lay upon mine and she screamed for food and sugar. In her shrieks of thunder I heard a whisper, "what if you lost a young daughter, who was prone to fear and falter, what if she were all alone in a world where beasts of all kinds were free to assault her, what could you do, if you were in not hers but another's water?"

"What could they Sarah, possibly for her alter?" "Nothing if she remained in her depravity, yet everything if she returned to her nursery, truly what is the worth of life if she is spent in agonizing misery." "Are you saying no life is better than a sufferer's?" "As surely as the serenity that pervades in the hereafter, professor." "And what Sarah, makes you feel peaceful are the surroundings of our departed cousins?" "Where sir, are the other worlds ailing sirens, its tightening irons, or its ghoulish lions? Had there been any of these earthly bindings, we would surely have heard of our brethren's horrific wailings. Their peaceful silence assures us they reside in gardens and mansions with no boundaries or railings and they laugh and play amidst lakes and mountains with no borders or ceilings." "And there are many in this world we live Sarah, who would say you live only your wishful dreaming, they would shout that their lovers cries they can still hear and those who have left are still with them here." "Scared they have been of death since an ancient day professor, have they not realized we harbor within, layers upon layers of fears. Content were we not, when dinosaurs tilled and roamed across our sleeping eye, when atoms collided to form universes in the sky, when sorrows never touched us and an everlasting peace never said goodbye." "Have you not heard, professor, of a sleeping child's gentle sigh?"

Passion

"I want to say something", he says in her ear, as they stand in the garden accompanied by the fountain's whisper. "Say it then", she replies softly, as she watches from a distance how droplets of water travel faster when approaching their sacred hour. "I am in love with you Sarah, I have been since many months and shall be for an eternity more, I ask for your hand today for a journey across each and every ocean shore."

As she stares into his eyes, she sees in the distance, the outlines of a murky abyss. "What happened?" He asks, "just for a moment I thought I saw vast dungeons amid lakes", she says, "mistaken I must be for my Jose knows nothing of life's pains and her aches." "Then travel further you must Sarah in my gorges and its wakes, keep going until you arrive at our very first kiss." As four eyes to each other smile, two dive deeper into the others ocean, wanting to see its vibrating colors and its rustic cellars. "What do you see Sarah?" "I see a cave Jose, murky and dark, it seems an eternity since anyone has been here." "How wrong you are Sarah, for it is my home in despair, enter now and I shall tell you a secret I have since ages longed to share."

And as she enters, she sees in the fading light, words carved in stone which when joined together, state Sarah a thousand times after. "Why is my name inscribed with such insanity, Jose?" "Because, when I am alone, you are my only fantasy," he replies. "Such pain, you feel, I could never imagine." "Such bliss I could peel I could never fathom." "You are surely in love, Jose, but only with a phantom, for what woman could give a man in a cave, true satisfaction." "Mistaken you are my flower, as for you, I would in seconds, entire galaxies abandon." "My heart feels beats, it never thought existed, where would I be today, Jose, if your love I had resisted?" "My heart would have denied, my mind would have cried and in my cave I would have soon died," "and yet, Jose, your tears would have never dried, for I believe that true love never unties, if there exist worlds and earths other than ours, surely the castles and caves in its oceans would bear signatures of their lovers sighs."

"Then give me your answer, Sarah, for the fish in my waters cannot wait any longer." "But I already have Jose, a thousand times each day, my feelings for you express what words can never explain, as I live each moment in ceilings, I cannot name. I am yours today and for every other, for when you are from me away I burn each second from the heat of our flame."

Needles

There are times in our lives when certain thoughts arise which fling us from paradise and into hell amid our innumerable cries, yet the same return us to our heavens when we ponder carefully on our most intricate sighs. The question of profound importance at such moments is whether our heart beats for the journey shall suffice, or if this is where the wind stops and our ascent to the stars she denies. Sarah glides across the interstate accompanied by oscillating waves of guitars and drums that tear into the heart and pierce through her mind. Sonic vibrations lift her soul, making it fly far and beyond, into lands of freedom, elation and liberation, where nothing is feared and all are divine.

Moments such as these arrive only seldom but when they do they are stronger and more potent than the oldest wines. In them this day are present a young girl and her car, both, together on a path that leads to lands afar. As she presses her foot on a lever, a plethora of feelings from nowhere appear. They ask of her why for the suffering only the few care why only for ourselves most of us fear, can we not spare, they say, some portion of our moments to wipe the Poor's tear? They circle across the length of the car, until they arrive at a gauge that foretells of their hour, a needle so light, that she might frighten her own is coaxed into rising beyond the fence of her home. Both she and the pedal when married together turn into a lions most dangerous feather, today, she may let go for a moment, a notion of sanity, much missing in our lonely dome.

Machines have a way of teaching us about life; they give us deep comfort when we are at times in the deepest strife, slaves they may be in their devotion, wrong they are who say they are devoid of any emotion. The sounds of her burn cry out at every turn, the songs of her delight play at every magical sight. Her voice shouts for those who wish to listen, her pain illuminated in every stroke of her piston. "I have adorned" she says "one form or the other, been through it all I have, one slaughter after another." "Your species" she cries, "continues to ravage every other, why", she presses, "do you feel you are forever?"

"Ideas", she says, "since the earliest have arisen, like my needle they have spread across different countries and nations, few have realized, as my two arrows surmise, they are choices that each of you can make which can halt this vicious tide." "Our screams", the needles say, "today, holds us in your gaze, yet tomorrow you shall forget and continue in your maze. We may be to you, slaves in our slumber, at our core, waves of energy we are, this you should always remember."

The Tune

Blues play in the background and gently melt away the heat of the scorching sun, this summer day trumpets, saxophones and violins from an old player hum a mellow beat tickling the skin of a young earthling. Music then remains a true friend of the ear, its whisper similar to shallow drizzle, which immerses herself into marshes, as earth and water mix in their passion to procreate a newborn layer.

Once in only decades does a tune come along that takes us along with her in the air, to places and palaces far and away where reside angels who know nothing except genuine care. These are indeed songs so rare, they lift us high and beyond our sphere and tell us there is nothing in this world or any other to fear. What matters most in these moments is the depth in the voice, for she keeps us mesmerized in her trance, until blinded she is by the harshness of our earth's glance. Jealous he is by anything which momentarily takes us away, for when we look at our favorite stars, the darkest clouds he makes sway.

By what measure then can we blame his day, only a blind follower he is similar to our fellow clay. Amused each second he is, watching us in our play, ecstatic he must be when we rush to slay. Yet amidst all his anger, even he must ponder on words that make him swirl on his axis a little slower. How were they born then, these vibrating waves through which we travel and luxuriate in surroundings so extraordinary, a lonely tree perhaps who was told she had the voice of a canary. An angel seeks in just such a song, a few moments of wonder, small surprise then that she finds within her heart, floods accompanied by thunder, for an escape to different worlds does not come without danger, yet the plunge we must take for otherwise we are nothing except rotting lumber.

Men and women are hardly alone in this endeavor, for objects both big and small live daily this dilemma, only a few amongst us are able to hear their whisper. Inside a house, dates gossip on a calendar, a watch clicks herself a little faster, a glass nudges to the waves a little closer, and a wall says to her sister, "This melody, we shall always remember". Outside in a garden, the tune humbles all, as it coaxes mulberry trees to fall and the sky birds to stall. The grass begins to weave and says to its inhabitants, "rejoice, for our day is here, be merry and happy, forget forever your every tear, for these moments to us are most precious and dear."

The Wise

"Have you ever wondered Jose how elements of our world never completely disappear, how they change only from one form into another, how the trunk of a tree is tortured and yet still survives for us as paper, how sheets of steel are cut to reveal a soaring propeller, how a gushing stream assumes the appearance of bottled water, how a butterfly grows and blossoms from inside a grasshopper, have you ever thought of memories that never sleep even when our eyelids end their flutter."

"True you are Sarah and yet who shall decide whether a different form is for worse or for better?", for I have seen days which arrive full of glitter only to appear some time after an empty crater, I have felt in tragic eyes, how feelings are delivered in the ink of a letter and I have been awoken in evergreen gardens and mansions, where a gust of wind has shouted, "my ire you shall always remember." "The truth is Jose, there exists in this world, both sadness and laughter. Look at the years gone by and you shall see in them, moments and hours when all you wished was to cry and yet look a little closer and you might see days and nights when life danced at your every sigh." "Are you saying Sarah, that both exist in our desire?" "I say only, that they reside in the care of the world we so admire." "I agree Sarah, that for most among us this is the reality and yet, there are people in our midst who are above misery, slavery and pity and live their lives in blissful fantasy".

"You are mistaken, Jose, for they have understood life's irony and decided to embrace her sea. They have lived in poverty, understood jealousy, practiced levity, and embraced our life's brevity. They live in caves and in castles, on mountains and on islands, in the largest cities and in the smallest towns and if they have a thing in common it is a deep care for humanity. Wherever you meet them they shall drape you in their civility and astonish you with their humility." "But, Sarah, what is the secret of their insanity, how are they this way?" "They share, Jose, a pattern of thinking, a way of feeling and of living their dreaming in the confines of our sphere." "My mind exists outside yours Sarah and I cannot understand what you intend to share."

"What I am saying Jose is that some among us have realized that life is short and she is nothing to fear, there are problems in life we can with the right approach bear, they have survived most of all, Jose, because each second of their lives, a smile is all they wear."

Murder

They say a picture tells a story of a thousand words, but can a few words tell the same of a thousand pictures? They must, Sarah decides as she strokes all of her ten pens to life, reprint they do a story from the morning paper, that talks of courage amid desire and a rebel engulfed in a fire. As her fingers slide on the keyboard, they begin to quiver at what they see, the sinister outline of a horrific murder, planned and executed with precision and thunder.

In the remote regions of a land far away, Sarah watches the soul of a young lover hover and sway. As the image becomes brighter, a young girl stands in tears, naked yet draped completely in red. "The pricks of their thousands of knives," her voice cries, "took from me my last breath, as I struggled to escape the angel of death, his eyes laid upon my helpless state and he lifted me in and said," You shall feel pain no more, as I hold you now in my arms, in peace shall you and I live together in eternal farms." "Today you awaken, a tragic tale of slaughter, for all I ever dreamt of was a life of peace and laughter, all I ever wished for was to become a loving wife and have a beautiful life."

"But why?" Sarah cries, as her fingers tremble, because "I did not shy!" The spirit replies, "from blaming, taming or tearing our love, from smearing, shearing or failing our love. It happened for my fall, in the heart of another, for wishing to share my destiny with my true love and not some other. Slain I was for my dance in the rain, for my songs in chains and my stance in pain." "Who was it that did this to you?" ten fingers ask in their sorrow? "Tomorrow, Perhaps", she says, for today you might not bear the answer." A wave of pain and anger engulfs the fingers, as the faint whisper of a terrible torture travels through the flesh and into their aurora. "Tell us now?" They shout in anger, the voice of a young girl screams, "my brother and my father." "This is insanity, the ten cry together." "This is reality", the stains of blood exclaim in perspire, "We live in a world very different from where you reside, many here like me are led everyday by our kin into the fire." "This is madness, the fingers sigh, where is compassion, where is reason, where is love, where is mercy from the heavens above?"

"When lives are lived in a box of tradition, there, one's own wish becomes the greatest treason," the shadows from an angel reply. "They tortured him for three nights and then cut out his liver, as they laid it before my eyes, I cried for days and told them we would remain forever, two logs in the same river. As the stars bear witness, in love, as in death, I did not wither." "salutations to your strength of character, as I bow to your love for your other, shame on those you see daily this fixture and turn the other way, proclaiming, what can we say when the aggressors quote their scripture, Who will fight for lovers slain, dreams maimed and hearts forever chained? Where are they who shall challenge those who say "but our honor she stained."

The Fairy

Alone on a lonesome road, her hair sails furiously in the gush, her face strains to focus on the breath of her sighs and a denim jacket begs to be torn apart by the air's rising tides. As she stops by the side to gaze at the amazing spectacle staring at her eyes, she is pricked in a thousand places across her body by the effortless song of a wailing moan low in pitch but high in intensity, she kneels to the ground to hear more intently and soon it appears, the soft murmurings of a whisper, "at peace, we are in eternity."

The whisper becomes louder and envelops her surroundings, burrowing deep in the hilly grasses in the shadow of the distant marshes, it shakes the leaves on the trees and makes much stronger the roots of millions of flowers with the utmost ease. Who is she?, Sarah questions, this woman who sings, whose vocals follow the stems of the earth to its core, awakening the very foundation of its ore, thundering through the breath of the valley, her presence oozing from the base of each living creatures pore. "I am a fairy, Sarah", arrives the reply, "I live in this moment in your fantasy, yet I promise you I am she, you call reality. I blow every second, a spiritual fog from my mouth, it contains elements of nature, you know nothing yet off, I have lived and seen all, from the time of the early plundering of the wanderers to the raping of the Indian villagers by their conquerors, this land is alive because I breathe into it, the fire of life amid a desire for the elimination of all strife. You may enter further, only if you bring to us, peace and harmony." "I live for nothing other, fairy", Sarah replies, as she gets into her vehicle and climbs into the vast wilderness of the mountain heights.

High in the valley, swaying grass on the hilltop glances adoringly at his beloved atop. As the sky guards preciously his lover, together they gaze at each other until greeted they are by a shower amid a wink from the weather. Soon arrives the roar of thunder and clouds of feathers fall into a deep mountain crevasse making both moan and groan with pleasure. As entities make love by the side of a river, "together, we shall remain", they both affirm, for ever and ever. "And is there anything young one that is left for me to deliver", asks the fairy from the young seeker. "Only, your story", states Sarah.

"It is enough for you to know, that I am never lonely." "Go back to land and let your kind know, there are places on earth that are still full of mystery, within them reside tales of eternity, love and serenity. All that is to be done is to replicate these sightings on faces and I promise that whosoever wishes shall make true happiness their destiny."

The Forest

A strange wonder it is that we think almost never of our evergreen forest. Forgotten we have how it was for ages our one and only nest. How then we used it for our game and rest and leaped from its plethora of trees to find suitors to impress, who among our billions will stand out and confess, abandoned it we have this day to the hunter's merciless zest. Would not tigers and lions today ask, "why now when we are scared of our own shadows?" Would not elephants and birds, question, "why, when you have so much more than your arrows?" "Would not endless fields of grass sigh on watching their receding meadows"," Would not oaks and barks cry, "if not us then spare a thought for our sisters, for acres upon acres of our kind are lost in their sorrows." Scream soon they will together, and state, "leave us in our home or we shall kill our young in their womb, no end there is in sight to your savage nature, no love you have left for any other creature, so much for all your knowledge and literature, no difference there is between you and an illiterate stranger, what did we do to deserve this torture, why steal from us our shelter, when we pose to you no danger.

What then, could be our answer, "wait a while longer and we might become a little softer" or "hide from us forever, as we cannot control our hunger." Neither will suffice as they have already seen our plunder. Millions of roots we slaughter each second and yet they seem to us only a number. There are then Michelle, many feelings I wish to bare. How can some feel, fluttering wings are still a prey, how can guns fire and their friends betray, how can bullets desire to destroy birds in their play. "Why do you think, Sarah, that so many go astray? For if all slaves followed their masters, species upon species would be in plasters.

Absolved we are not of the crimes we have committed for It is not merely that animals and forests we have neglected, the truth is entire kingdoms we have each day devastated. In lush marshes and lakes, dungeons amid craters we have created and in green pastures and innocent village's pure mayhem we have initiated." "Are we brutal killers then Michelle, or merely unrepentant sinners?" "How often do we think, Sarah, of a chick's pain before we slash her skin in our dinners? If you order a killing from lands far away, guilty you are of murder, no matter how much you pray? A day arrives when her screams haunt you no matter how much you delay and in your heart you know truly what she felt no matter what you say."

Fur

Rarely is it in our desire for the same that we break free from earthly bonds to live in our flame. Where are those faces, those gazes, those places that would make us with passion and fire, exclaim, "Today, we have touched, what we have always wanted to tame." In the middle of the sunshine state's belly, lies a space still breathing that air of wilderness, untainted by invading hordes, it harbors its existence in a wind of unique stillness. A town surrounded by lakes in the middle of which lies a small airfield, its rugged beauty, unspoiled by innocent birds descending gently in its arms to be forever concealed.

A shadow of white envelops Sarah as she moves closer to a paradise of fog and water. High above the earth and in the midst of gathering clouds, she pulls on her companion and says circle we must now, as we maneuver through the air through which we plow. As she completes her turn and tugs on the reins of her stallion, he responds gently settling into his rhythm, as he does he enters an even wider blanket of thick fog and clouds, gently buffeting against the rising air that brushes his hair and blunts his stare. As the whisper of his hoofs gets lighter and lighter, the blanket of soap starts to get murkier and murkier, inside an angle's innocent heart now, alarm bells ring louder and louder.

She calls aloud to the elusive strip of land, "where do you hide?" She asks, "I mean you no harm, I promise to touch you, as would a feather, grace you as would a lover, caress you as would a tear and lace you with tiny squeals of my stallions leather." "Never did we ever hesitate to show our beauty to those who bravely contend with our weather," say white bands of feathers, "yet angels we do not let pass, until they feel our tremor, as the sky is our witness, we harbor a spectacle to remember, amongst our plains reside waterfalls and lakes, upon them recline ducks and fish of all sizes and shapes, surrounded we are by five ponds of desire, enough to soothe the staunchest hearts fire, such is the magic of our heaven that at times even the devil stops from afar to admire."

As tears form in a young girls eye, wiped they are furiously by the billowing winds, as her plane turns to ask why, clouds gather to state, "only in his arms, are you allowed to cry." She looks up to say goodbye to the sky, and shortly after, cradled they both are through the pit of a handsome clouds thigh, a tremendous shudder greets them as thundering shrieks of a giant moan pierce the sky, as a giant cloud lets out a satisfied sigh, his minions falter in the background and a dazzling mix of green and blue from below says, "welcome Sarah, cherish this moment, for only a few do we allow to float in this view," there are in this world certain places only, where we would want to live for eternity.

The Gaze

"I am the fire, the seer and the admirer, at times what I see in this world, is nothing except the core of my every desire, at others, the many faces of an illustrious liar, yet to feel its wind, to breathe its grass and to steal a glance, I would never tire. I look at her not as she sees me, if she only she knew, I too can see. I feel her presence, as I feel for her essence. She sees in me a lonely abode, I see in her, contradictions untold, is our world then, only a glorified urn? I look nearby and I see beauty and the sea, yet the further I gaze, I hear poverty in its plea. I live in a garden and I play among the swings, just once, if I could, I would fly high in the sky, aloft with my wings. A block of wood I am, stuck on a patch of green, lie on my throne Sarah and together we shall be alone and free. Similar we both are, living not in the tale but watching from a distance. Present and yet lost, content on never leaving our fence. "You speak of some other," she says, "for they say a bench in the park can see more than millions in a lifetime ever will. And yet, we are different my handsome bark, for I live in this world, and I see beauty in its twirl, and while in her misery, there lays an untold mystery, in every moment of creation, she arrives, a new reality for my salvation, each new second is draped in fascination and each new day harbors melodies and songs of a different sensation."

"And yet you live nothing," the voice of a young daffodil, speaks aloud, "for when I sit close to a rose, my shadow flirts with his and both of us together make the most beautiful prose. In this moment we are one and the world stands dazed at our symmetry. The scent of our bond travels far and beyond our humble flowers, trees or lakes, for since the first dawn we have lent to true lovers the purity of an emotion they name ecstasy.

And yet you live in delusion, speaks at last, the goddess of the forest "I see in this world, nothing that amazes and nothing that fazes, I see no beauty and I see no misery, I see no light as I have no sight. I have lost the sense of pain, as I have lost the sense of shame. Since the dawn of time, I have been misused, since the advent of our cosmic rhyme, I have been abused. With death and destruction, have they burnt my soul, with blood and friction have they damped my cold. You call me grass and say I am green, yet I tell you today, my eyes are shut from what I have seen. Men and women, assembled and slaughtered, trampled and tortured, murdered and butchered, for what except ideas that are anything but serene."

Thoughts

"Do you feel Sarah, that witnesses are required when two hearts collide? That signatures are required before two birds can take flight, that documents must be signed before two swans can glide? Do you think as do nations to our left and right, that pens can charm and fates decide?" "No! Michelle, how can true love be scribed on printers and papers? How can feelings be described in court house letters? How can a third decide when come together the souls of two feathers?"

"They proclaim Sarah, that desires must not be fulfilled until arrives a certain hour, that fires must be tamed until the two bow to the church's power." "Do they not realize, the mere glimpse of a lovers eyes are a sublime delight and the parting of lips themselves a heavenly ride, the mind along with the heart defies how so many still think this a matter black and white when all can see the joy of the wind when she caresses her beloved kite.

Priests and rabbi's are unnecessary when two egos have died, of all the great things that have come on our earth and left, love remains with us still and the air attests that she has never lied. Think they do not of flames that rage among those in love, for when a girl casts her rob aside and her lover soaks in hills and valleys inside, then a cosmic heat melts away an earthly pride and even planets and stars to each other confide, circle no more, for we must loan to their passion, a longer night."

"What of lust then, Sarah? Should we indulge in her whisper or hide forever from her shelter?" "Have you seen Michelle, how the cold air from the arctic comes to us rushing in winter, how she nourishes us with snow and blankets us each December. What would we say if we never saw this side of our weather? Who would then play amid logs of a white river, to whom could we say, we are cold and thus much closer to each other. Lust like love, is the breeze from afar, day and night we are told it inhabits the Satan's tar, yet the truth is greater than an ancient prison bar, for lust is passion and passion is desire and desire is the feeling and our feelings reveal the strength of our emotions and their meaning.

"But Sarah, they are two different things, how can you say they are one and the same," "because Michelle, lust as love knows nothing of blame. When we were born, along with all the others, she came. How can we now banish her to a chain? True there are times when she lives to her fame and yet in most she brightens and enlightens our every flame. Thoughts and intents decide when the cold air comes alone in a storm and passes by merely chilling us in her wake, or when she arrives accompanied by her calms welcoming us to her lake. Go beyond your libraries and dictionaries, go farther than the coldest northern cities, travel to the deepest and serenest valleys and you shall rename a word much derided in our societies."

Droplets

What does rain think about our kind before she falls? What does she feel just before she kisses the floor of the earth and crawls? What are her emotions when she is growing in a cloud and thinking about our ponds? What could be her passions when she prepares to drop among our lawns? How many stop to feel her shiver? Would she ever care about where she lands? Would she ever ask for permission before she touches our sands? Nothing except grief she would feel Sarah, after she has tasted our soil and caressed its walls, her innocence would shatter upon learning of our history, her seas would part after they learn of our savagery, once she glides past our minds she would scream for sanity and after a while her heart would beg the sky's for mercy.

"Are we really so tainted Clara, that floating flowers would touch us and blow away? Or so callous, that showers which grace us would go astray?" "Words are without meaning in certain places Sarah, just as sentences are without feeling from certain faces. Such is our condition today that for our leaders and their utterances, men and women are ready to slaughter other kingdoms and their princesses."

"Perhaps Clara, there still remain cities and nations among us, where people are free from prejudice and malice, where every home is for its inhabitants a beautiful palace, where people live without fear and a calmness surrounds the airs, where elephants have no tears and the sea praises the sky and her layers, where dogs smile at strangers and kittens study the lines across their fingers." "I fear you speak of a different universe, Sarah, whose denizens say the same we are no matter what our colors, the blame we place on others we must first find in our own feathers, who say we are all one no matter where we are born, together we are no matter which oath we were made to sworn." "And yet Clara, so many I have met in my journey who harbor the same thoughts, who say coerced they were at an early age when little did they know about themselves or the world, and day after day made to swear allegiance to maps and their curls." "Forced into silence such entities are Sarah, even if they are alive, as

94

entire continents are swept away in an oceans tide." "And what do we say to those on the crest, Clara, who claim they are free. The whole forest laughs when such claims are made by a tree. It asks our kind about how many stop to feel her shiver? How many gaze at her in winter? If only, the forest says, Sarah, we could see her pain in the flow of a river."

Designs

"Have you noticed Sarah how everyone here is smiling? How they are for everyone's attention vying? How with chemicals and curls they are their own reality denying? Have you ever felt that at events as these, people are watching others but themselves admiring?" "Is it true that to keep on surviving, one must engage in a little lying?" "Michelle, the fountain of youth, lays within and not outside and yet an image shown to the world, we cannot from our soul hide. When rituals are performed for beauty and form, our hearts know we care about our worth and wish our journey to prolong." "Why grow old at all Sarah, why if our genes are afraid of their dying do they not extend their sighing."

"Because Michelle they are gliding for us only to hear our newborn's crying. Uninterested, they are in the length of our lives, in the health of our eyes, or in the manner of our demise. Careful they are, though, of a pregnant woman's cries, for within her lays their ultimate prize." "I am still at a loss, Sarah! Do you mean our wishes act on nothing except their advice? Our hunger for beautiful daughters and sons are nothing but lies? Are you really saying our desires are nothing except a roll of the dice?" "Michelle, the world is an eternity more mysterious than what you and I may surmise and things which may seem obvious hold more secrets than the sun's daily rise. Look at life through only one of her lenses and you shall pass through her without feeling all her different senses.

Have you never wondered at the design of a man, how he can still father children even when he can no longer till his land. Have you never thought of the burdens of a woman, how she goes through pain to bear the birth of her adoring sand. Have you not felt in their faces, wrinkles and twists when they are past the age of clutching tightly an infant's hand? Have you not seen them pray at this time for a magician's magic wand?"

"People, it seems Sarah are afraid in our world, most of all of their mortality." "Unaware most are Michelle, we are dead for a few hours each night, awakened only by our earth's gravity, for in our dreams we fly far and away to gardens, lakes and oceans in another play, only to return in the morning and state what we saw was only insanity. Ponder not on bygone years, or on eternal fears, Michelle, live your life, in all of her moments and you shall feel when you die, none of yours but only her tears."

Rain

Have you ever thought of the feelings of a cloud? How she basks us in her shroud and screams her greetings aloud. Have you given any thought to her flakes of sorrows, how they moan when they turn to beads of rain in our meadows. Have you heard the tone of her wail, when she watches a dying whale? Have you felt her anger when she sees men and women on earth die in hunger? Have you seen how her feathers flicker when they hear men powerful and proud whisper, when by a stroke of a pen, wars and battles they trigger, when they say we are special and the rest are only litter. Have you felt her pain, when her droplets of peace fall on nations and populations insane, when her sighs have fallen in vain and warriors proclaim thousands we have for our leaders slain.

Have you ever dreamt of what she must live through each day as she watches our worth each moment decay. What she must think of our clay when she watches us revel in our favorite play. Have we thought of how she gathers from afar each day, her seeds and plants them in her womb so we may have our treats? Have we ever spared a moment at the discomfort she feels when she bleeds, how she makes sure, we quench our thirst even when she is without her sheets? Have we ever asked her of her needs?

Who among us then shall console her in her grief, grace softly her delicate reef, are there voyagers between us present who shall cajole her as a branch caresses his adoring leaf? "Let her answer then our questions this summer, for her fate as ours, hangs on her murmur," a million voices cry, as mothers, brothers and forgotten lepers look towards the weather. "Forgotten you all have," she says, "I am of the same elements as you, why then do you feel emotions are only true for you? I swear by my neighboring sea of blue, I have moments of solace very few. Live amongst you I have for millions of years, so lost they have never felt, each and all of my layers. Strange creatures you all are, for I cry at times each day and still you cannot see my tears." "But how can we believe that you have purpose in your desires?" She is asked, "Have you not seen me drown your raging fires," she retorts, "How I have calmed you in your forts and charmed you in your boats."

"What can we do, to bring to your altar, happiness and laughter?" "Smile at each other, and end your vicious slaughter, from Alaska to China, people at their core, need only shelter, food and water."

The Abyss

Some say currents of electricity move across our world faster than light herself who travels at a speed much feared in our time. They say thoughts in our midst are stealthier than the curves of a dime. They say feelings cross continents and oceans more fiercely than jet engines can climb. They say emotions inflamed can in lands far away inflict a horrific crime and yet what do bygone years say to men and women once they are past their prime? Loved me you did when I was with you in bliss, when you felt your first kiss and when nothing in your life was amiss. Why this hate for me now, when you knew all along, temporary it was this journey of yours in this abyss.

"Did you see Sarah, the state of him in his story, how his eyes lit up, when he saw in our sighs, fascination in his glory? How when we first arrived, he barely shifted in his seat to shed us a glance, how we had to sing and dance to break his trance, how his spirit lifted suddenly when you spoke of his beloved France. Little did we truly understand of his tales of gunfire and bravery, yet something from his past we gave him as a gift when we listened to his sails towards Normandy."

"Maybe, Jose, someone to talk to is all they require, as they spend almost all their waking hours sitting idly by the fires. Maybe, if nothing else, some can stop by simply to hear of their lost desires and lend a few widened eyebrows at real or imagined admirers." "What will you say Sarah, to your last hours? Will you fear their powers or welcome them with flowers?" "Life, Jose, is a gift both bitter and sweet, some say a bit of sugar we taste when we feel ourselves breathe, others contend, sadness stalks us in every beat yet it just may be that fields upon fields of canes may wait upon us as our coffins are sealed." "And maybe Sarah, this is just your fantasy? Maybe deserts and droughts are what welcome us when we write our last page. Maybe what you say, is just a dream you had once of an idyllic village."

"What do you think Jose, ice feels when kept for years in a freezing cage? Have you never thought of her joy when freed she is in old age, how she screams with laughter as she proclaims, for a while only I was stuck in a fridge, see my beauty in my sleep now, as I have left forever a prison of rage. Death is reality Jose, yet far from the severest penalty, there are times in almost everyone's life when they feel, tear apart they should their belief in immortality. When she arrives, she does in some rather suddenly and at others hesitatingly, if there is anything she decries it is the pain she inflicts as she guides us to our sanity."

Bubbles

"Have you ever thought of the strangeness of bubbles floating in water? What they must think of their host as they dance in her river? Have you noticed how they smile when they glow at each other? How they at times merge to become one after they caress and glide into another? How they look to us the same and yet different they are to each other? What they must think of us, as they say, despite our differences, in our world we all come together? When shall we realize, a perfect son, daughter, husband, wife, or friend this world of ours can never deliver? And yet in this ambition we turn away, our closest, as they wish to taste life in a separate flavor. Do not expectations kill joy, when she is among us from January to December? Is it not unrealistic Clara, to have none, from our dearest in summer or winter?"

"A lesson I learnt some time ago Sarah, was that happiness for our kind lies in seeking weather a little fainter. When heat bears down on us from May to September, we pray to the sun to burn a little softer, when cold arrives and surrounds us in her desire, we yearn for a flame to turn ever more brighter and yet think, of the time in between, and you shall remember, sceneries, fantasies and serenities depicted on the canvass of a thoughtful painter.

Recall Sarah, the other day, when we slept by the side of a lake, how when we opened our eyes, the tide touched our feet and left a gift for us in her wake. I feel our lives too resemble her shape, do you remember her changing currents, her gushing waterfalls and beautiful swans?" "I do Clara and I understand now what you mean when you say, things which flow, do so singing songs. For the merriest in life are those who understand, cherish and nourish her aches. Some time ago, Sarah, I knew someone called Nora, she faced in her life, obstacles we cannot begin to comprehend and yet with glistening eyes she embraced them all as a force inside her said to her, this and every other challenge we shall defend.

Victorious she was not in aspects considered important in our day, for never an hour did she spend in splendor or in play, yet she attained a harmony in her life, for which most today would be ready to slay." "How Clara?"

"She became a wave Sarah, in the lake of life, flowing with its currents and diving in its falls, glowing in its storms and caring for its logs. She is a swan in the pond Sarah and a few days ago I named her Nora."

Electrons

A strange thing happened yesterday Sarah, working on my paper I was when out of nowhere appeared jagged flames from an electric switch, at first I thought merely a circuit was torn, only later did I realize how my judgment was wrong, for as they leapt across the room in their games, one said, "only a few hundred years ago you would have said, our existence lies only in the mind of an eccentric witch".

What happened then, Jose? She asks, "as I looked at one deeply" he said, "amazed are you not, that I speak to you this way, just think of how our misery as imprisoned we were for millions of years without our play." "Shocked I was to see that they had so much to say, for they burdened me with their tragedies until my head began to sway". "Different they surely are from us Sarah, as they are from a separate clay, yet so similar to our stories theirs seemed, as each wished he could simply fly away." "True they are Jose, for if it wasn't for a few brave souls some time ago, those in power would have never allowed are sciences to grow, as our world languished for decades upon decades in an ignorant abyss, electrons frozen in captivity are free today to tell us what they missed."

"They say nations upon nations resisted attempts to harness their power, as they cried incessantly from their torture, they said over and over, we wished that your kind had minds a little broader." "When we roamed the savannah Jose, it made sense to seek familiar patterns and shapes, when we roamed the jungles in small groups and tribes it was understandable that we were fearful of all other apes, no sanity remains in such ways now, as the last century has shown, progress yields only to peoples and countries who seek and immerse their interiors in varying colors of different drapes."

"As they flew across the room Sarah, some said many of our kind still harbor feelings of dread from what they are not aware, they feared mistrust, rivalry and a dogmatic adherence to a fixed ideology might again lead humanity towards total despair, they said look forward we must towards each new reality, as within her armory might lay, the cures for our continents of poverty." "I often wonder

Jose, why we don't in our hunger yearn for new discovery, when was the last time you heard, new potions were found, which would lead a deranged to a full and complete recovery." "Before they subsided to disperse Sarah, they reminded me of how some of us are full and yet still are hungry, they said, change we must, those who offer the forgotten nothing except only a few words of pity."

Decisions

At times the weight of this world feels a great burden, especially when people that matter turn into feelings uncertain. Indecision then at this time is for us necessary to abandon, a great distance there is between dying at our lonely tavern or flying to space and beyond the rings of Saturn. When the light in our lives assumes the life of its shadows, then inside we must look first to understand the world of our sorrows. Too often our finger points outside, failing to see a part of itself that it has burnt. Fear which drives us to admonish the other, neglects to inform us, that it is her we must tear. Love too disappoints us, when she assumes we must all be artisans of the utmost care. There is a different dress that at times we must wear, it must be devoid of cloth so that every action of ours is bare. Only then can we read the truth and slash the self so it can shear.

There is nothing to fear Sarah, for at times even an angel can err, go to him, say the waves of the ocean and the tears in your eyes shall forever disappear. "He is going away," says Sarah, "this I cannot bear, can he not see in me the pain I feel, does he not in the least bit care. "Go to him Sarah and greet him in this darkness with the smile of a burning lantern, you will feel soon, that while the self may be small, the heart is wide just as the gorge of a great canyon." She gazes out at the roaring sea, its breeze caressing Sarah with the songs of its plea.

"What you say is pure and true, if he is to one day be mine, he will surely return in time," is her reply to the endless blue. "You are an innocent flower, Sarah," the waves cry again in unison, "what you do not understand is that he is already yours, you seek possession but in true love there is only freedom."

I understand now what ripples in water have for an eternity begged to say for often it is that our desire for another is only about our own fire and yet true love does surface when we push aside ourselves and become some others admirer."

Sayonara

Goodbyes invariably arrive amid the sorcery of the wind and the sky. The clouds moan as they cry in the wetness of their sigh. More often than not, tears are formed, but remain forever within the home of the eye. They say something is broken when a lover leaves for a land afar, it must be time which hurts the most as she slows down in silence waiting for an eternal hour.

As the magic of a thousand nights spent in the other's arms appears before their gaze, "our love for each other, you must always remember", a circle in each of their eye says. "A small journey before you leave we must take together, two prisms of light say to their other, for soon you shall be far away and every second to me will feel like forever.". "And yet I shall return before your eyelids return to each other in their flutter, for my heart shall refuse to beat until it hears your whisper, he replies.

As she closes her eyes and sinks deep into his arms, he takes her on a journey through deep forests and jungles, upon vast mountains and their valleys, beside towering glaciers and their rivers and beyond mighty oceans and their islands, until they stop by a lake where a young mother glides merrily in its waters with her swans. "Here", he says, "we shall share what we may never have wished to bare." "And will you be ready Jose, with whatever appears?", "anything, Sarah, except your tears".

"Do you recall, Christmas, Jose? When we were lost in the north and never could find a place to stay, what happened in the car made every pore in my skin fill and sway for I swear by dawn I was shivering in the rain of our play." "Travel with me Sarah to when we cuddled by the fireplace every second of one night, how till the early hours of dawn we saw the waves swim past her tide, as you lay in my arms at one moment I cried, when the water rose to show me two hearts had from the earth untied." "And do you Remember Jose, the day which erased all fear, for a gentle kiss on my forehead made me aware of how much you care, how in those seconds of despair you pushed me to dare and said fly we both shall across every layer in the air."

"And never shall I ever forget Sarah how we used to dance in the afternoon rains, how we felt the rhythm of each other's veins and traveled together to the distant skies and their plains." "Goodbye, Jose, she says at last, take care of yourself and in moments which are bare, spare a few thoughts for a broken feather."

The Log

"We are too busy in our lives, aren't we? She asks of a flame as she stares at the center of a blazing fire. Worried forever about our careers, goals and hopes, bound by our hundreds of daily chores and surrounded on all sides by a thousand closed doors. "Are our lives not bound then by a million different ropes?"

"Even more are they Sarah who fret each second about their innocence," says a block of wood as he burns, "Imprisoned they are in ideas that have flooded through their shores, taught they were at an early age, think not with your mind, listen only to your kind and true happiness you shall surely find, if the elders could only see, they have raised daughters and sons who can see and yet still are blind." "Explain further what you mean." "Laughing I am at my fate, for you seek my advice at this moment yet only moments ago it was when you thought of me nothing and threw me in her arms to bake." "If only I had been told you see us naked and more," replies Sarah. "If only I had known that you dream of things true and pure. If only they had said, care deeply for a tree, as her scars have understood our world since years before, never would I ever have indulged in a thing so impure and yet as you leave us now, forgive a young girl and her cold and state your feelings aloud.

"Dreamt of many things your lot have Sarah since they declared a truce with the bears, since they felt the emotions of their tears and since they understood the meaning of pairs. Passed through generations of newborns they have their fears since a hundred thousand years. Tell your friends and as well as your enemies, nothing is permanent and nothing is for certain, no man is forever another's servant. Seek happiness not in thoughts chained; instead seek it in gardens and meadows amid flowers just after it has rained. Go to the ocean and talk to her waves, after a while they shall know you are they are harmless and shall hoist you amid their layers. Visit the skies and she shall scare you with her screams yet stay for a while and she shall show you her dreams. Become one for a moment only with a gust of wind and lose yourself you will in ecstasy and laugh at the innocence of your sins."

Distance

"Shall a time arrive Jose, when our love shall look at and us and proclaim, two entities for sure I did on earth claim? Will she shower us with her petals so we look to the world separate and yet to her the same? Would she sprinkle our path with roses so gardens and their butterflies could feel our flame? Could she then state, that there are two on this land who live in moments which have no name, who touch each other as the grass caresses his rain, who sense in the others eyebrows each and every pain, who need only the billowing winds to make love again and again?"

"Have you ever been Sarah, to the valley of kings, where reside rivers, glaciers and the most beautiful springs, have you felt there the presence of unearthly things, such as the leaves which never stop their songs." "Daily do I travel Jose to such places on your wings, scribbled my name onto your arms I have, for they are my eternal fins." "Then we journey together already amid majestic sky's and stars Sarah, for love can never be a destination, it is the precious hours we spend in our very own tower, the view you seek from above is already present in each and every corner, look carefully and your heart shall sense the scent of our flower."

"Oh I do Jose and cherish it I will for many lifetimes other than this, all I wish to remember is how intense we felt when we first graced each other's lips, for my thirst for your breath is as undying now as it was when we first met, if only you would allow a lost lover her forgotten sips." "How would you know Sarah how I have wanted our earth to stay, to stop her dance and neglect for a second her play, how then I could say, create a way for my love and I are hundreds of miles away." "When will you come Jose, for the cloud without his vapor is like mud without her clay?" "In the morning Sarah, wake up at dawn and walk in the garden amid a rising star, when you slide then by our oak tree you shall feel me, even though I am in lands afar." "Miss you even more I will then Jose, for the moments we spend alone each day shall never come again." "And yet they should never be in vain Sarah, for love only grows when forced apart, just as poets scribble trees with prose when someone rips their art."

Screams

"What is happening sir, to the blades of an engine's compressor? What do they feel as they slice through the air and make her wither? Are they sad for her some time after, or elated forever at her shiver?" "Extend the throttle as far as you can Sarah and let us taste for ourselves the wind's tremor." As her hand thunders to life an old Cessna's liver, they see rushing towards them, a gust stronger than the fastest sprinter. "Can you see what is transpiring Sarah?" "Well sir, we are traveling much faster" she replies with a smile, "and is that all? Can you not see in her rush a yearning desire, tell me Sarah, that you see at least that her heart is burning for a taste of her lover's fire."

"This is so strange sir, for I felt forever that horribly burnt she would be from entering a box we so admire." "That she does Sarah and yet such is her love, that she would rather taste a flame and bake for a few moments in its ire, than live untouched for years and become a denier." "And what of those on land sir, who one day wake up and say goodbye for today and ever, if there is anything left to say, it shall be said on paper, who say unhappy we both shall be if we continue to live together, who say mistaken we were when we thought we lived in the colors of the same feather, yet if they could only see, sir, how a gust adores her visitor, how she dissolves in his arms as if he were her last supper and how she is crushed when he leaves and passes her by for another."

"The wind like life Sarah, flows on even though wrecked she is in her heart by a thundering desire and yet on land, men and women are unwilling to listen, even as their beloved scream their lack of fire." "But what of those sir, who say, together we are in this life and every other, who say we shall not change in sadness and in laughter, who say never shall we break our bond as we are one forever." "And what is forever, Sarah? For all we know, the next moment could herald a fatal thunder.

Promises of eternal love are no different than those of eternal lives, both start in awe, delight and surprise, only to suffer later from a horrible demise." "I think sir, that your heart is broken," she replies as she looks for the hurt in his eyes, "for how can you think of true love as transitory when you just felt for the roaring wind, such incredible pity? If love in our world was only temporary levity sir, then never would we be hearing at this moment her shrieks of insanity."

Choices

"Have you ever awoken from sleep and felt, at a great distant you are from the qualms of this world? Have you ever been submerged in work and suddenly dreamt that you are on an earth where different norms have unfurled? Could there be towns, cities and countries among our ever growing galaxies where defection is earned and convention is burned? Where parents are interned and children concerned? Where animals are heard and their ideologies learned? How often do we stop to think of these things as with each passing day, another page of our story is turned?"

"Almost never Sarah, do we halt to ponder upon the words inscribed in our journal, it is as though humanity remains convinced, she is a species eternal." "What you say is true and yet most would reply, that they see amid themselves or others no scribbling pens, that they have on this earth or others many friends and no need there is for them to look through their lives through a deeper lens."

"The people you speak of Sarah, live their whole lives inside of a fence. Misguided they are if they think I talk of stencils and inks, deluded they are if they feel angels roam the skies memorizing their sins. Look if only once, carefully at life herself and you shall see for yourself how she looks at each and grins. Shocked she is at our ignorance, when some say, written down already she has each soul's story in the skies inn's, laugh she does in pity, when she says, if nothing else, ponder at least on the infinite choices I give you each moment, both in your smile and in your wince." "But is it not true, sir, that at times sadness decides to invades our lives, that tragedies arrive, and take away our will to survive, that dreams certain to come true in younger years, later bow in subservience to life and her accompanying fears."

"You misunderstand my point, Sarah, for I never once claimed that she is simpler than the designs of these stairs, all I am saying is that once imprinted, it is for us to judge whether we see one or all of her layers. Life is similar to a fast flowing river, beautiful and scenic in some parts, yet treacherous and insensitive in others, if her water glistens by its banks in the evening, than at some distance further, she is sure to have in a flood some innocent screaming. What you must realize is that you have decisions to make so long as you are breathing. Just as the night turns into day and the summer to his sister gives way, sadness is followed with laughter and joy is swallowed by pain, and yet happiness and misery exist only Sarah, if they are felt by an observer, your attitude is your pen, your choices your paper and the sum of them all shall become your book when you die. The difference only is that you create it as you go along, in your hands lie your triumphs and your shame, fate died long ago when she said, I shall remain no more, as I am too easy for you all to blame."

Ashes

A very different day it is when clouds of darkness hover over the innocence of angels, time herself cries when she realizes she is late and cannot stop the insanity of certain vehicles. As the stench of wreckage fills the air, birds and crows scream with horror as they fly far and high in fear, a tree in the corner flays its arms as it sees in the rising smoke a new reality refining its shackles. Soon, the wails of familiar sirens surround the meadows and a few souls gather to search for life amid death and her shadows. Yet all they see are two boys asleep, tangled in steel and spread across the wheel.

"What happened?" one asks the other, "Flowing already they are in a different river", arrives the answer, "are you sure you cannot feel even a shiver?" he asks again, "not even a whimper but at least they are together," remarks the stranger. As officers arrive shining their badges and torches, they ask of the men, "who first appeared". The first one answers, "a dark cloud sir, for he begged us to leave before the two young lives he teared." "How?" they ask, "in a flash of lightning sir," the second answers, "For she blinded the driver, before he could turn, just as some women are draped so they can never earn." "Where is the cloud now?" "They ask, "Gone she has with her rain to torture a fairy, for when she learns of her lover's story, scream she shall until the universe returns to infinity."

"In the cinema of life," the first says, "must such films be shown, where loved ones die and the rest are left to forever cry. Daily do we see thunder in all its different forms, if only a cloud could feel but once the plunder of its storms," and if our jails are filled with rapists and sinners, then surely the sky too harbors a few murderous pillars," replies the officer. "And yet you all misunderstand," commands a loud voice from the far reaches of the sky, "for those who wreak your peoples and nations are only felons who escape from my many dungeons and cellars, never would they hurt even a fly if on your earth resided only dwellers relishing their winters."

"And yet if you kept them in chains we would still have our brothers, if you hadn't taught them haste, young girls would still be with their lovers." "Surely, you must know, I have only so much control over my weathers, for now, let one know, her Jose reclines merrily on a patch of green surrounded on all sides by a thousand orchards."

Blinds

"What do you feel when birds glide past your railing?" "I look towards the sky and ask where was I failing?" "What do you say when ships are sailing?" "What can I share, when I can only hear the waves breaking?" "What do you think, when the leaves are swaying?" "I wish to drown in pools of ink, so the world can hear my aching." "What do you sense, when you hear children playing?" "I yearn for sight, so I could cherish their cheering?" "Who do you curse when fall is approaching?" "Whom can I, when old books to me mean nothing?" "What do you hope for as you talk to your sighing?" "I wish for a world, where pain is dying, where tyrants are crying where elephants are flying, where cynics are admiring, crows are rhyming and love is binding."

"Then you desire a planet that is forever shinning Michelle." "Tired of my own life I am Sarah, gone with the rains have my hopes, my sighs, my dreams and my cries. You and others live your life with lust and vigor, how many times have you thought of our pain and begged the sun to burn her torch brighter."

"Our star Michelle is only a lover in a daze and our rock is nothing more than his latest craze, inside of it lies nothing except empty space and yet like each addict among us, he shall grace us with his light so long as our earth intoxicates him with its luscious plays." "And while she twists him with the charms of her face, is there no one amongst you, who can lend me their gaze? For I wish to see the jungles of Africa, I wish to flee the bears in Alaska and wish to plead with the snow in Antarctica, like you Sarah, I too once dreamt of becoming a voyager." "And you can Michelle, remember adversity and hardship has no friends among our kind and though it seems as though before we were made, a pact with her was signed, men and women weaker and poorer than both you or I have stood their ground and demolished her pride. While it is true that you cannot see me today, you can touch my skin and say what you may. The most beautiful sceneries are those Michelle, which are created in the mind. Think of those, who have there, nothing except a dark blind."

Lessons

"What have you learnt so far in your journey Sarah?" Waves ask of her as she reclines by their side. "Only a little so far" she replies, "for mine is an infant compared to your story. If lessons are to be learnt, surely they should be dug from the trenches of your history." And what makes you so sure, deeply informed are the droplets in my armory?" "Because I am here only as millions before me were cradled in your cavity."

The ocean grows in size, swells with pride and hastens its ride until it reaches a voyager soaked in its tide. "We have traveled across the world to different countries and continents and yet a goddess we never found who understood our song's melody. Speak more of what you see and we shall bow to our new majesty." "I see ancient animals as I peer through your drapes, I feel the presence of strange creatures as I gaze upon their shapes and I dream of a world vastly different as I part through your waves." "And is that all? Is there nothing else you shall tell us as you stare at our world through its layers?" "I also sense sadness, more than you ever felt in those days."

"Bravo! Young girl, for it seems you have stumbled across our tears. As your kind live their lives oblivious of our fears, little do they realize, they have lived in our care for millions of years. A forgotten mother I am now, as your billions are content with their prayers. Daily do they plunder my body, polluting it in their insanity, do they not realize, I still harbor within my belly, so many of your brothers and sisters? And then they wonder, from where arrive tsunamis, for if my love for your kind has been pure, so have been my scissors." "A mother surely then you cannot be, for which today would enslave so many of her own to such slaughters?

True you are when you say man is destroying his waters, for I have often thought of what one thinks as a whale's throat he severs? And yet your vengeance is equally brutal, as pity or charity your might hungrily devours. True it is that we were bred in your womb, yet you forget how we have developed and grown. We understand now how we are your son and your daughter, just as we have wept when faced with your thunder amid your laughter. This is the truth

118

of your life as every other's, varying weathers you have at times even for days in the same Septembers. No different are we, when at times we are to ourselves unknown strangers. The more I learn, the more I feel, no one is perfect as no one a failure, we only live moments as they arrive, wrapped in their distinct flavor."

Pain

"Strange is this life Clara, in which we lose those we love faster than the trees do their leaves in the fall, night after night I ask the stars why they do not at one time, take us all?" "Why would they ever leave a planet bare amid its wall? Sarah, whom would they watch then as there would be no one left to brawl? Why would they drape the only light nearby with a dark shawl?" "Why my lover? Under whose wings should I now seek my shelter?" "No one else's but your own Sarah, for you are and always be a fighter, if nothing else cherish deeply the days you shared with him and remain in love with all of which you remember." "I always shall Clara, and yet who shall comfort Sarah, when she cries through all of winter?" "No one except her tears, for they shall dry long before the next summer, life must go on precious flower; she awaits none and in the end shall betray even her own shadow."

"All Alone I feel this day, what shall I do now that I have no one of my own." "And yet you have your passion and your tone, Sarah, travel the world on foot or glide through her streams on a raft, seek happiness in yourself and let the earth again see your laugh." "But an adventure Clara, we already began, when crying we left an adoring cage, how could we have known, at that very moment, we were thrust into life and onto a stage, without scripts or rehearsals we opened our new born lips, sinking forever into begging for an adoring glimpse."

"And do you remember when they tore into us, instruments and machines awaiting our screams, if they had only known, they poke young girls who shall have earth shattering dreams, if only they had been told, there are some you hold who shall part the mightiest seas."

"And yet today I feel that I live on an ocean, but without its breeze, that I roam the forests, but don't see any trees, that I talk to myself, and yet find no ease" "remember, Sarah, sadness has many souls to freeze and she can any one person only for a time appease, surround your soul in sceneries different and soon she shall forget she had any illness." "In the morning I am in peace Clara, as I

practice daily a regimen of stillness and yet even as I do, I see sometimes floating beside me my flower, every minute of the hour."
"Smile at him Sarah and let him know you are safe, the irony of life is that we fear most for those who die, if only our millions realized, those who have left, worry not of theirs, but only of our sigh."

Adi Khan

Infinity

Today I felt as I have never before, sailing in the air I was, with my ship and her ore, never had I dreamt that I would feel this pure, just me and my sail in the wind amid its lure. Into the endless sky we fly, both haunted by the thought of a return from this high. If gods and goddesses recline in this heaven, verily the song of my innocence may for a while play in all seven. If angels and fairies can reside in this vast mansion, surely there must be room for a young girl and her stallion. They sing these songs of love and joy as they caress the waves of the deep sea of the sky, soon however, her ship shall say to her she is thirsty and both shall have to return to a lie.

"Wait", says a cloud from a far, "before you step down into the depths of your world, you must unfold a story untold. Let your people know that your roof resides within her heart, a vicious devilry. Let them know that they are at the mercy of forces that initiate murder, instigate mayhem and enforce suffering. Like every other, in this universe, the sky, just as the ground, assumes for a time only one of her many faces, she cajoles you today with her graces, tomorrow, she may not and you may suffer from her gazes. Be careful of what you love so deeply Sarah, it may hold for you a story very different from what you perceive of it at this hour."

"What do waves do when the winds have drifted? What can one say, when a mask is lifted? Since forever I thought we lived amongst a virgin, imagine my surprise when I found rape inscribed in her intentions. All this time I had thought she was pure, little did I know she was so much more. Who would have thought she had evil in her midst, who could have fathomed, there were swords in her mist?"

"And yet you sail my seas, just as a gale does when seeking the winter breeze." "I do, for when I sail between your layers of blue, I find peace, just like grass after he is kissed by his beloved dew. When I roam the white feathers gracing your thigh, I feel a certain calmness, only darkness knows when she closes an eye. When I glide past your tears, I feel emotions, I never believed sighed."

"And how does a young girl traverse the earth with such conflicted feelings?" "Just as a sphere that rotates between night and day, accepting, both are at all times at play."

Love

"Never did I ever think Jose that you would leave me one day, never did I dream of a play whose curtains would be torn away, whisper if you can hear my shrieks today, for my feelings have so much left to say." "Then share whatever you may Sarah, for I feel your pain as she traverses her day, if only you could see your lovers tears, imprisoned in the depth of an oceans bay." "What if I were to travel Jose, upon the breath of the sun's ray? What if stars millions of years across were to collide together to form a way? What if I spoke to the earth and she agreed for her spin to delay?" "And what if dinosaurs appeared again Sarah and began to slay? What if galaxies by the thousands collapsed into a fray? What if the clouds descended forever to melt into clay? Think of a thousand different stories we can Sarah, the truth is, the laws of your world, mine refuses to obey."

"Bolted I am Jose, by a hundred locks from all sides, how can I ever forget when our ties are cradled in the warmth of my eyes." "The denizens of my new reality Sarah, tell me something of yours, they say a true feeling experienced has its own cries and yet some we must be let go, as each that remains does so at a price."

"The inhabitants of your worlds may be wise Jose, but how do they explain a young boy's demise? Have you never asked them why some oak trees live for hundreds of years but one among them suddenly dies? Night after night Jose, I dream of our sighs, only to look towards the sky and ask her a thousand whys, can I not borrow you only for a few hours just so we can hold each other and cry our last goodbyes." "Strange are the meadows upon which I glide, Sarah, for I seem to travel through vast distances as fast as beams of light and yet so near I am to your heart still, that I feel on my face the scent of your each and every tear." "Everywhere I look Jose, there are signs and signatures of your care, everywhere I go, my heart asks me why is he not here?"

"And yet I am, Sarah, I am beside you when you sleep, I caress you when you weep and I take you in my arms when you cannot breathe." "How can you Jose, when you are in a dungeon so deep?"

"Stars and planets may seem to us at a great distance Sarah, when love is true, they come much closer and are barely an hour. Sometimes I feel I live amid the light's stare as she blazes through each moment across your air, once when you were sleeping and I was feeling your hair, she said to me, "a pity it is that they are not aware, if only they knew, we are always so near."

Visions

"A strange dream I had the other day Clara, I dreamt of a man I have thought of many times before, walking across gentle sands he was along the Caspian shore. As he moved towards the sea, I saw myself captivated by his charm more and more, not until he swam into the tides did the ocean scream. A ghost only it was that I saw, hallucinating in sleep I was only, her still waves swore."

"How far were you from the water, Sarah?" She asks, "Only as far as a mother is always from her daughter Clara and yet deeply troubled I am for while it is true that our eyes at times deceive us in this world, never would I have thought that our minds would shield the oceans from her crimes." "What did he look like? Was he someone you knew?" "His face was vague and yet when I was searching his for clues, I felt a familiar scent which said, we had once shared a beautiful view, it said the both of us had sailed for years on layers of blue and hinted together we both had imagined a life different and new."

"At times Sarah people who are close to us leave something behind, when they are far away we see their signs when hours turn to years and minutes seem like days." "Who would have thought that I could be this way, for loneliness was for those who are of life's beauty unaware." "Feelings of any kind Sarah, one should always be ready to share, for they are the petals of love that lead swollen hearts to tear, even queens of joy and laughter have their share of pain, great actresses they are, as they hide their sorrows in their dances in the rain." As smiles appear and display their care, one angel says to another, "Then you feel my king I miss Clara, or is it something more that is amiss?"

"Lost you are in the memory of your first kiss, wander you will aimlessly along your castles pavilions until you break free from its gates and search for a handsome prince. The waves are there only to help you break free from your past, they hide his soul only so you can be complete without his grasp, their towering tides beg to understand, roaming empty dungeons is like walking through gardens and forests wearing a mask." "How true you are Clara, for never would I have thought that I would become this way, since we decided to climb different stairs, locked in the same tower I have been all this time, thinking he would return in tears.

How would I have faced my fear if it was not for your presence here, surely they do not lie when they say, sisters are infinitely more wiser than how they first appear."

The grain

"I am so much more than a bowl of cherries, fields of strawberries or intoxicating curries, in different colors do they come, the petals of my billions of rosemary's. Have you not noticed how I drown some in endless worries while others I let play among my angels and fairies, yet only a mirage this is, as I have planted both bliss and torture in each and all of their stories. Having lost your closest you may feel today that you are alone, yet know that the greatest of victories are at times gifted to those who overcome their tragedies. Just as from nowhere appeared a twist in your tale, know that this is my game and I play it as I sail, just as you fear night after night you shall hear sirens of a hail, this is my name and you shall scream it in your wail, just as it disappears, the haunting of this gail, you shall know I am life and I have never worn a veil."

"And yet uneven are your different arrows, just as grieving are sinking shadows, even a child would say, some you treat as hunted sparrows while others you greet as the greatest pharaohs." "People of earth, Sarah, are on different steps on each of their ladders, who would wish to see each day, the wax burning from the very same candles? Who could possibly want to hear, night after night, hymns and praises of unearthly laurels?" "And yet suffer many from your battles and your quarrels, if it were not for your horrors, you would have had today, many more sons and daughters."

"And maybe Sarah, I have enough already, for have you seen how the sun bakes the earth and shrinks her waters, how the forest burns and silences all doubters, present I am this day in insects and her quarters, in mammals and their laughter's." "Wondered for a while I have, why you showed me your beauty only to snatch it away and proclaim it was your duty, what could a young girl have done in her journey that distant lights were to her shown and then extinguished so cruelly?" "Taught you I have Sarah, that the flame you saw burnt inside you, just as the brightness that glows surrounds you, seek not in another, your joy or your pain, feel only in yourself your passions amid their rains and as you grow you shall realize I too was once only the size of a grain."

Layers

There are times in life when a few moments arise which decide in their midst what is to become of our lives. Sometimes they come without warning, like the sudden appearance of snowy weather, at others, they announce their departure, so that we might brace for a stronger winter. The key to both is to recognize them without fear, for these guests of ours seldom stay for supper. Success in life does not equal happiness and yet her magic provides a window through which we can peek at our Everest. The mermaid of opportunity surely rises from her lake to touch each soul's destiny, yet silent she remains always, embracing only those who understand her naked symphony.

This day, the engine of a Cessna shall have to decide whether a young girl has seen enough of life to attain clarity. As it starts its roar across the runway, it gathers speed until its arms beg to be lifted and its face yearns for its beloved wind. As he is cradled into her charms, an old instructor watches a young girls each touch and stroke with the precision of a hawk. Long gone are the days when he shouted orders on the battle field, when the air whispered of bullets and their cries and he had to hear in its shrill his dead soldier's sighs, and yet to this day he shall rate each aspiring flyer only by the passion he sees in their eyes. As she maneuvers her bird in different positions and postures, asked by her foe she is about her visions and their futures.

"What is the difference" she asks of him in reply, between thieves and caregivers? "Luck amid their signs", he answers, bewildered. "Nothing of the kind, she replies, for in life, "we have in all places both grievers and achievers". Locked now in thought is an old pro at the game and yet even he is left wondering when he let go of his queen. "Differing attitudes we have among our peoples, Sir," she says to lighten his pain, "some can let go, in heat or in rain, whereas others are left tearing their every vein, how we define life is all we need to understand the length of our chain."

For a few moments silence hugs the tiny cockpit,. soon after she hears a loud voice boom from across, "Congratulations Sarah, for you have conquered these layers."

Adi Khan

The End

The Virgin Sky

www.ingramcontent.com/pod-product-compliance
Lightning Source LLC
Chambersburg PA
CBHW060438130626
46555CB00005B/2410